OTHER BOOKS BY C.K. MARTIN

DIRTY LITTLE WAR

TAPAS AND TANGELOS

TEDDIE MCKAY SERIES

THE CROCHET KILLER

A TASTE TO DIE FOR

LAZARUS HUNTER SERIES

BLOOD INHERITANCE

TAPAS

AND

TANGELOS

C.K. Martin

No part of this publication may be reproduced, distributed, or transmitted in any form or by any means, including photocopying, recording, or other electronic or mechanical methods, without the prior written permission of the publisher, except in the case of brief quotations embodied in critical reviews and certain other non-commercial uses permitted by copyright law.

All the characters in this book are fictitious, and any resemblance to actual persons, either living or dead, is purely coincidental.

CONTENTS

The tangelo is a citrus fruit hybrid of tangerine and pomelo or grapefruit. The size of an adult fist, they have a tangerine taste and are juicy at the expense of flesh. They generally have loose skin and are distinguished by a characteristic nipple at the stem.

CHAPTER ONE

Hayley tipped her head back and let the shower's tepid spray rinse away the last of the soapsuds. She checked her arms one final time for splashes of paint before turning off the water. It slowed to a trickle and then continued to drip onto her right shoulder. That would be a job for Pablo to fix another day.

She stepped out and despite the heat of the day, felt her wet skin prickle. The sun still shone bright and fierce, but once night fell, the breeze would do its magic. Soft and gentle, it brought with it a calm to close the day. Hayley loved this time of year. It was still quiet and relaxed. From the end of July through to early September, the days would be too warm and everywhere buzzed with tourists. Since she had moved here, even the locals had stopped taking siesta, caving instead to the demands of a twenty-four seven clientele from the cooler parts of Europe.

There were still a few more weeks before the frenzy happened. Weeks during which she could continue to enjoy the sunshine and slower pace of life. It was certainly better than being back in England with its rainy days and grey skies.

Through the open window, the smell of meat sizzling on a barbecue drifted in. Hayley suppressed a smile. It was Pablo's attempt at an apology food for his new guests. If you could call them guests. At the moment, it was a tenuous bargain on both sides.

She'd warned him not to advertise that the new - and only - backpacker's hostel in the small Spanish resort was ready for business until it actually was. He'd told her it would take time for word to get out there. There would be no problems. He'd clearly underestimated the power of the internet.

She couldn't help but feel sorry for him. The old building had fallen into a state of complete disrepair when the previous owners became too old to maintain it properly. The first time he had taken her to see it, after he had already completed the purchase of course, he had thrown back the doors and she had stepped back through time.

The traditional thick stone walls kept the building warm in winter and cool in summer. Something the previous owners had relied on as Pablo came to discover, when the basic water heating system failed to spring to life. It was the first of many problems the old building had thrown at him, but he had persevered. No problem was really a problem in Pablo's eyes. It was merely something that he would get round to fixing. Eventually.

Still, despite these non-problems being largely of his own making, she had caved when he begged her for help.

His mistaken belief was that people would call ahead to make a booking. Then he would tell them, apologetically of course, that they were full. A small lie until all the repair work was complete. Instead, he had been surprised by a knock on the door and the arrival of a young man with a strong German accent asking for a room for the night. Pablo had been forced to send him away to the main strip of the resort and call in a favour with one of his friends who happened to manage the front desk at one of the hotel chains there. That had kicked the renovations into high gear and Hayley had answered the begging call.

As she stepped into her shorts, she noticed a splash of bright white paint just above her knee that she had been unsuccessful in scrubbing away. She rubbed it again with the rough towel until most of it came off. Without a mirror in the room - another to do item on Pablo's list - she could only hope there wasn't any on her face or in her hair. At least the water had remained warm enough until she finished her shower. She hadn't been able to tell if Pablo was joking when he warned her it might not.

She walked through the main hallway of the old house towards the large open space at the back. To call it a garden would be an overstretch. Perhaps, once, it had been, but like the rest of the house, the previous owners had failed to maintain it. A few olive trees, gnarled and twisted from the wind that pressed the island's coast in winter, had stood their ground. The rest of the space was nothing more than the dusty, burnt orange soil that covered much of the island, hiding the dark volcanic rock below.

Despite the poor landscaping, the view was beautiful.

She understood why the old couple had stayed there long after they were capable of managing the property. Set high on the hillside, a single-track road swept down to the old fishing village to the right. To the left, the natural bay that attracted the tourists and holiday companies was gearing up for high season. From way up here, it was possible most of the time to pretend it wasn't there. Directly ahead, the ocean spread out, still and flat; its gradient from turquoise to inky blue making it picture postcard perfect.

'*Cerveza*?' Pablo asked, handing her a bottle before she could accept or decline. The beer was chilled and she took a grateful sip. 'Nice view eh?'

'It's beautiful. The whole place is. Or it will be, once you actually get it finished.'

'We make good progress, no? Two bedrooms. Two bathrooms. That is all we have left.' He shrugged to indicate it was no big deal.

'Plus the rooms on this side.'

'Small detail.' Pablo dismissed and took a pull on his beer. The three guests he had accepted got their rooms at a bargain rate. Faced with the alternative hotel prices, they had been more than happy to stay, even if the amenities weren't going to get the place a five star rating any time soon. Pablo's good-natured way with people was part of a smoke and mirrors act; his kindness made them overlook that there was only one working shower. The lack of air conditioning would be bearable for now, but in the middle of summer, even Pablo's charm wouldn't be enough to keep people cool.

'I think your meat is burning.' Hayley pointed at the smoking barbecue, where the meat was changing from cooked to charred. 'And I'm starving.'

'Of course. You must eat.' Pablo grabbed her hand and pulled her over to his makeshift cooking station. She smiled at the backpackers who had gathered on an old bench to look out over the sea as they ate. They were already onto a second bottle of inexpensive local wine, a relaxed look settling on their faces. She could understand it. It was why people came here.

Hayley was almost tempted to sit with them. Instead, she took the plate of meat and rice Pablo had piled high for her and began to tuck in where she stood. It was basic, but it was good. If he was doing this for them everyday then it was obvious why they were happy to stay in the half-finished hostel. 'This is good,' she said in between mouthfuls.

'It is nothing,' he waved her away, but she could see he was secretly pleased by the comment. 'I think I might stay here.'

'I thought you were going to get someone in to run the place?'

'Maybe. Maybe not. It is so beautiful, no?' He tossed another piece of chicken over the coals.

'It is.' It would be a lie to disagree. Of course, she knew he wouldn't stay around once it was complete and the days became routine. Pablo always needed something new to capture his attention and keep his hands busy. The view would only keep him contented for a while. Then it would be off to the next project.

'Um, excuse me?' A voice from behind them made them both turn around. She didn't say a stereotypical *g'day* but the Aussie accent came through loud and clear. Hayley saw a young woman in shorts shielding her eyes against the setting sun. 'Is this the hostel?'

'*Sí, sí,*' smiled Pablo, warm and welcoming. Hayley thought she saw a hint of panic in his eyes. 'Welcome!'

'I couldn't find the reception so I came straight through.' She gave a bright smile and Hayley resisted the urge to tell it was because there wasn't one yet.

'I am the manager.' Pablo threw his arms wide to denote his full ownership of the building and beyond. 'How can I help you?'

'My name's Kate Lanthorn. I've booked a room here?'

'Ah yes. Miss Kate. I remember.' He turned and gave Hayley a smile that she knew from years of experience meant the exact opposite was true. He had completely forgotten he was expecting another visitor today. This meant, of course, there probably wasn't a bed made up for her. This would be interesting. Like a cat with nine lives, he would make his way around the problem, but it was still fun to watch.

'The dormitory is almost finished I'm afraid, but it is completely fine to sleep in. We are running a little bit behind schedule with some of our repair work. But do not worry, for tonight I cook a meal for free to welcome you.' He pointed to the barbecue as evidence of good faith.

'Sure thing. But I booked a room. A double, not a dorm?'

'The double?' Pablo faltered and recovered quickly. 'Ah yes. The double. Please, sit with the others and help yourself to food. To wine. I will just go and check your room is ready.'

Hayley chuckled as Pablo practically sprinted back into

the building. She knew for a fact that the double room was not ready for anyone to sleep in it. It was where she had dumped her belongings earlier that day. She hoped Kate was aware that in this part of Europe 'double' often meant two singles pushed together anyway. It was likely to be Pablo's saving grace this evening. She looked over Kate's shoulder for signs of a telltale boyfriend. None had appeared.

'Hi, I'm Kate.' The young woman dropped her backpack gently to the floor and gave a half wave.

'Hayley.' She realised that between the plate and her fork, she didn't have a free hand to extend. She opted for a smile instead.

'Is that guy okay?'

'He's not the most organised, but he's a good man.' She snuck another look at Kate. Her light brown hair was tied loosely back, bleached almost blonde from constant sun exposure. She had a healthy outdoors look that Hayley didn't see very often. The tourists who turned up for two weeks were usually lobster-red as they tried to cram a year's worth of sunshine into fourteen days of hardcore exposure. Instead, Kate's face had a few cute freckles on the bridge of her nose and her exposed shoulders were a soft caramel colour. Hayley forced herself to look away and back up to those eyes.

'As long as this is a genuine backpacker's, and not some dodgy serial killer place. That's always the risk with new ones, isn't it?' Kate leant in and placed a conspiratorial hand on her bare arm.

Hayley resisted the urge to step away. Her stomach lurched with the dangerous territory. Breathe, she told herself. Just breathe.

'I guess it is. Wine? Food? Wine?' The words came out in a rush. She moved closer to the barbecue and nodded that Kate should join her. 'Pablo would want you to help yourself.'

'No worries.' If Kate had seen something in her eyes, she showed no sign of it. As she filled her plate, Hayley chanced another glance in her direction. The fading sun bathed Kate in flattering light. That was all, she told herself. It was better to ignore the fluttering in her stomach. A distant memory, the feeling of attraction, was released for a moment before she put it back in check. It was a momentary lapse of emotion. That was all.

Hayley swallowed. 'So, will your, erm, other half want a plate as well?'

'Other half?' Kate looked confused.

'The double room?'

'Oh, I always get a private room when I go somewhere new. Most places don't do singles, so I ask for a double. Didn't even think about it. I'm here alone.'

'Oh.' Danger crackled in the air. Whether it was from the admission that she was a woman travelling alone or from something else, Hayley didn't want to examine further. 'I'll be over there then.' She hurried over to the table to join the others before waiting for a response.

Perhaps it was tiredness that made her weaker than normal. Or the paint fumes that had messed with her head. But as Kate piled her plate high and walked over to join the group, Hayley felt her heart begin to beat in time with the swaying of her hips.

#

The evening settled down into a convivial atmosphere after the sun set. Despite his lack of forward planning in every other area, Pablo had lights strung up in the outdoor space, bathing them all in a soft glow. It was just bright enough to see by, but dark enough that Hayley could sneak glances at Kate every now and again. Every third time, or so it felt, she would find Kate looking straight back.

Hayley knew she should stop drinking and head home. Her friendship with Pablo only obliged her to be here for so long and that time was up a few hours ago. When he had finally been persuaded that everyone had eaten enough, he had finished cooking and joined them. He had lit a handful of citronella candles in brightly coloured glass jars and set them down on the table. As he told them wild stories in broken Spanish, for the first time Hayley could see his vision of what the hostel would one day be.

If his guests were expecting some kind of backpacker's party atmosphere, then they weren't going to get it here tonight. Or perhaps ever. It wasn't really a Club 18-30 tourist trap even in the main part of town. Over the years, she had experienced some of those youngsters in her bar, looking for a good time and finding no one to have it with, unless they happened to find grey-haired retirees attractive. Or married men who had somehow managed to leave their wives and kids back in the hotel room after a busy day at the pool.

Pablo had assured her that businesses in the resort were on the up and up. She hoped he was wrong. But seeing all the faces here tonight, she conceded it was nice to have something new in town after so long.

When Kate had returned from being shown to her hastily assembled room, Hayley knew she had decided to stay after all. A strange sense of relief had hit her and she tried to convince herself it was just happiness that Pablo was able to keep another paying customer. She wanted him to do well. Wasn't that what friends were for?

As Kate flashed her a conspiratorial smile, it became harder to lie to herself.

Instead, she listened to the chirping of cicadas fill the air as the others around the table compared travel notes. They all seemed so young and yet so experienced in comparison to her. She had lived in England until she arrived here when she was about their age. She hadn't moved on since. The town had become her home. The furthest she ever travelled was to the main city in the north to complete bureaucratic paperwork. Even then, she only stayed long enough to get it done, have a coffee and a bite to eat, then return home. She was not the travelling kind. Being settled meant something to her.

Everyone at the table had been to Australia apart from her and Pablo. He shrugged when everyone else had agreed enthusiastically about a particular town. Three out of the four guests had also been to Thailand. She had finally realised that was where they were talking about, after they'd listed an itinerary of exotic sounding names. Hayley had looked at the ocean and then back at Pablo. She saw him smiling at her and knew he felt the same way. Why travel the world, when you had all this right on your doorstep?

The wine continued to flow throughout the conversation. A young Tempranillo, effortless to drink.

Hayley had paced herself, knowing she had to get back down the hill and to her own bed. She could see the lights twinkling in the darkness when she stood to get another bottle of wine at Pablo's request. The others had not been so cautious. Although they weren't rowdy, the Swedish girls were slurring their words and eventually stood up to carry themselves off to bed. Pablo followed them inside - possibly to protect his freshly painted walls from their stumbling - and the other young man at the table stood up and followed too, wishing her and Kate goodnight in a language that certainly wasn't English, Spanish or anything else that had its own dictionary.

Hayley watched as Kate leant back, resting her hands on the bench and turning her head up to the stars. 'I think I like it here.'

'It's a beautiful place.'

'We're lucky to find it before everyone else does.' If Kate was as drunk as the others were, then she wasn't showing it. Hayley knew that Aussies could hold their drink. She hadn't had this much herself in a long time, despite her best intentions. It had been too easy, with Pablo topping up her glass and the casual conversation flowing around her in the warm air. One beer was her usual limit. Tonight she felt her inhibitions begin to fade away and it both excited and terrified her.

Besides, it was easier to watch Kate if she was hiding behind a wine glass.

'I'm not sure this place will ever be a tourist hotspot.' If it did she would leave, thought Hayley, but there was no need to tell Kate that. 'Besides, it would probably ruin the town.'

'I think you're wrong. Over the next few years, I think this will become a really popular place for people like us.'

Hayley felt her face scrunch in confusion. Maybe she'd had too much of Pablo's free wine herself. What did 'like us' even mean? As she was about to ask Kate if she had the strongest gaydar in existence, it dawned on her what she really meant.

She thought Hayley was a backpacker too.

Hayley let out a bark of laughter that was met with a look of surprise. At thirty-six, Hayley's days of backpacking would be long over, if she'd ever had them in the first place. She was about to correct Kate when the young woman continued.

'Don't get me wrong, I love Thailand. Travelling all over Asia was one of the best things I've ever done. And it's way more affordable. You could get a whole apartment in Chiang Mai for what I've coughed up to get a room in this place. But you can't just stay in one place and say you're travelling, right?'

'That makes sense.' Hayley decided she liked it when Kate talked. Her strange elongation of syllables that defined her as uniquely Australian was easy on the ear. Her words were clearly enunciated but that didn't stop Hayley from watching those soft pink lips move in the semi-darkness.

'Besides, it's easy for us Aussies to stay over there. Getting to Thailand or Indonesia isn't too difficult. We had family holidays in Bali when I was a nipper. But Europe? That's the next destination for a lot of people I know.'

'Europe is the first destination for people back in

12

England.' Hayley couldn't help but point out the obvious.

'Which makes total sense, right?'

'It does.' Hayley smiled at Kate's passion and enthusiasm. She'd clearly caught the travel bug in a way that had never made sense to Hayley.

'Hey, why do I get the feeling you're laughing at me? I know a thing or two about this stuff.' Kate's indignation was feigned.

'I'm sure you do.'

'I've been on the road for nearly three years now. As soon as I finished Uni, I took a gap year. Haven't been home since.' She obviously wore her wanderlust as a symbol of honour. Perhaps in backpacking circles that counted for something.

'Not once?' Hayley wanted her to continue talking while she did the calculations in her head. That must mean that Kate was twenty-four. Twenty-five at the most. No surprise then she was still filled with youthful exuberance. It was sweet.

Cute.

Hayley pushed the phrase away and forced herself to stop staring and listen again.

'No way. This is all I want to do.' She looked up at the stars and Hayley assumed she wasn't talking about Pablo's. In its current state, the hostel was nobody's dream.

'I can certainly think of worse ways to live.' They might not be on the same page, but that in itself wasn't a lie. Why else would she be here permanently herself? The alternatives paled in comparison.

'Anyway, that's enough about me.' Kate turned to her and by the dim light gave her a smile that added about a thousand watts of its own. Hayley's heart did a double beat. It must be the wine. Speaking of which, Kate's glass was empty.

'Can I get you another?' Hayley asked, pointing to the glass.

'Sure, thanks. Just one though, yeah? I'm still struggling to get my body on the right time zone. London was the worst.'

'I would imagine it's quite the difference.' Hayley said it without thinking. If Kate picked up on her inexperience when it came to travel, then she didn't say anything.

'It's not the time difference that's so bad. The hours flying hit me the hardest. I always get the cheapest flights, but you can bet your arse they're the worst times. It always takes me a few days to shake it off, you know? Thanks.' Her eyes were on Hayley as she topped up the glass with an experienced wrist.

Hayley tried not to squirm under the appraising stare. Leaning forward to pour, she was hotly aware of Kate's eyes glance down to her chest before coming back up to her face again. Pablo was yet to return and she was beginning to wonder if he would. She hoped that the Swedish girls weren't throwing up over any of the walls she'd helped to paint that day. There would be hell to pay if they did and she wasn't sure it would be Pablo cursing them or her.

She knew she should leave. Kate's glance had confirmed what she suspected about the young woman's availability and potential willingness.

The two of them out here, soft lights, wine, and no one else, was dangerous territory. Hayley had avoided putting herself in this exact position for years. Tonight had somehow snuck up on her. A slippery slope she had believed she was fully in control of, but now she could see that she'd fallen down in her own denial. When Kate started talking, telling tales of her adventures, it had been too hard to walk away. It was a life Hayley had no interest in living herself, but that didn't mean that Kate couldn't tell a good story.

It wasn't just her stories, Hayley admitted to herself. It was that Kate seemed completely at ease with herself in a way that Hayley envied. Her lean, tanned legs were only partially hidden under the shortest of shorts and when they had accidentally brushed against Hayley's own during dinner, it had felt like her body had burst back to life in a tingle of sensation.

Kate was smiling at her from behind the wine glass and Hayley realised she'd been staring. Shit, that was not how this was meant to go. Kate was pretty. And charming. And so, so interesting. But she was completely off limits. Hayley could come up with enough reasons why to tick off the fingers on both hands. She was one of Pablo's guests and that was the lie she would tell her if Kate decided to kiss her.

That was an egotistical assumption, she reminded herself. It had been so long since she'd been flirted with that she was probably misreading all the signs anyway. With almost a decade between their ages, she could hardly claim to be fully up to speed with the lingo of twenty-somethings.

The reminder of the age gap was a whispered voice in her mind that she wasn't a predator. Nor would she allow

Kate to make her cross boundaries she had set in stone for herself.

'Do you know anything about the stars?' Kate asked suddenly, looking up again at the sky.

'What?' Hayley was confused. Why would Kate be asking her about the stars?

'Those things. Up there.' Kate nudged her playfully. She didn't move her body back away before she continued talking. Hayley could feel the heat of her. Too close. Closer than she should be. She should move.

She didn't. Instead, she followed the line of Kate's arm as she raised it and pointed. 'Your stars are different to ours.'

'I'm fairly sure stars are stars. We don't get special EU approved ones over here.'

'Stop being cute,' Kate flashed her a smile. 'Your constellations. They're different from the ones I grew up with. You have the North Star, we have the Southern Cross. I've always been fascinated by the skies.'

'I know nothing I'm afraid.' It was true. Her nights weren't filled with stargazing. Such a thing seemed so child-like and foolish, she'd never even considered it until now. They were always just above her. With Kate's body pressed alongside her own and the stillness that surrounded them, she could suddenly see the appeal.

'Let me show you.' Kate pointed at a star that hung brighter than the rest. 'Can you see that one?'

'Yes. The big one? Is that the North Star?'

'No. Most people make that mistake because it's the brightest. It's actually Polaris. The dog star.'

'The dog star sounds way less prestigious than the

North Star.'

'It's because it's the key star in the constellation of Canis Major. It means Greater Dog,' she added by way of explanation.

'I see.' Hayley wasn't really listening. She could feel Kate's breath tickle her ear as she talked. They were closer than they needed to be for this conversation. Common sense told her to pull away, but her body refused to move.

She felt Kate's arm slide around her back and brace itself on the bench so she could point to the sky in a way that was more closely aligned to Hayley's line of sight. 'The constellation goes from here,' she pointed, 'to here,' her arm retraced it's movements an inch or two, 'to here and then over to here. Can you see it?'

'I'm not sure,' Hayley confessed. She'd been concentrating more on stopping her body from shaking.

'Let me try again.' Kate's arm slid down along her own and cupped her hand. 'Extend your finger,' she quietly instructed. Hayley did as she was told, her traitorous mind wondering if Kate gave such explicit and detailed instructions under the sheets.

She allowed Kate to lift her arm to the sky. Her eyes found the bright star again and the two of them aligned her hand so she was pointing directly at it. 'Perfect,' Kate whispered and Hayley could feel her lips almost brushing her cheek when she spoke. Inside, a part of her that had been frozen was turning into a molten core with each word Kate uttered.

'Now,' instructed Kate, 'move to the next bright star on the right.' She pushed Hayley's hand over, and intertwined their fingers as she did so. Hayley's breath involuntarily hitched and she knew Kate must have felt it. 'This is where you start. From here, back up to Polaris. Then you slide your arm down,' she slid her own arm down along Hayley's forearm as she did so, 'to here, here and here. It's not quite straight, but you can see where they are if you go straight down.'

'Uh huh.' It wasn't actual words or sentences, but it was the best that Hayley could do. Her mouth was dry and she didn't trust herself to speak.

'Then you move back up just a tiny bit until you find the previous star. That's the spot,' she held Hayley's hand in position for a moment. 'Exactly there. And then you drop down and right to this one here,' another movement that seemed to push their bodies closer together as Hayley's arm moved further in front of her vision. 'Then you slide out all the way over here.'

Kate moved her arm further to the right. She could feel Kate's arm beneath her own, the soft naked skin of her bicep pressed against the side of her breast. The thin material of her tank seemed a flimsy barrier between them. The contact seemed to last for minutes as they sat there, pointing at a star Hayley knew she wouldn't be able to find again if she tried.

Not that it mattered.

She turned her head to ask a question, say anything that would break the unbearable tension that was growing inside, but found her face less than an inch from Kate's as she did so. Kate was looking at her, not the constellation. In the faint darkness, she saw a tongue dart out across dry lips and she wondered what they would taste like.

She felt Kate's arm slide the rest of the way down her

own and then down her side, grazing the curve of her breast with the back of her hand as she did so. It rested there on her waist as she waited for the world to implode as the stars above her once had.

This was her last chance to pull away. She might not be a genius, but she knew what would happen next if she didn't.

Hayley hesitated a moment too long. Kate took the stillness as permission and dipped her head down, pressing her lips against Hayley's own. They were soft and tasted of warm bread and herbs mixed with berries from the wine. They yielded under the slightest pressure and then Hayley lost herself in the kiss, all thoughts of why she should or shouldn't be doing this disappearing somewhere on Kate's tongue.

She reached out to pull Kate in closer. Kate's stomach was simultaneously soft and hard under her palm, warm through the thin material of her t-shirt. Hayley tugged at the hem, needing to feel the skin against her own. It had been so long since she had touched someone this way it sent her into a mindless delirium of desire.

At first contact, Kate groaned into her mouth, a sound that reverberated down through her body and towards her thighs. The desire it sparked overrode the warning that her brain was trying to send. It wasn't too late. She could still walk away now, before this got out of hand.

Then Kate's hand wound around her neck, nails slightly scraping the nape, just below her hairline, sending a shudder of undisguised lust through her.

She was lost.

Hayley wanted to be closer to the body in front of her.

Wanted to be pressed against it in a way the picnic table wouldn't allow. Kate must have felt it too, for she muttered, 'are you in one of the dorms?'

'What?' Hayley was yanked back into the real world for a moment. If she were to confess anything, now would be the time. Kate took the silence as confirmation.

'I have my own room. Come on. I need to get out of here.' She grabbed Hayley's hand as though she was scared to stop. That if they hesitated for too long, then the magic would be broken.

Hayley allowed herself to be pulled along. The words of protest died in her throat.

As they moved down the darkened corridor, the rest of the hostel was in silence. Pablo was nowhere to be seen. Hayley was grateful. She knew that if she saw him, he would be a reminder that she shouldn't be doing this. For his sake as much as hers. Kate was, after all, one of his guests. In the darkness, Kate fumbled in her pocket for the keys uninterrupted. She unlocked the door and pulled Hayley inside.

The only light in the room came from the large windows on the far wall. It was light enough for Kate to lock the door behind them; a presence of mind Hayley wasn't sure she herself possessed.

Then Kate was pressing against her, pushing the lengths of their bodies against a wall that Hayley had painted herself only a few days before. If she'd known then that the first action these walls saw would be her own she would have scoffed in disbelief. Yet there she was, pressed up against the coolness of stone with the heat of Kate's body providing a delicious counterpoint.

'I don't normally do this,' Kate said. That was the kind of thing you said if you did it all the time, Hayley knew, but it didn't matter. Kate's hands were pulling her tank top off, eager to get to the skin underneath, breaking their kiss to remove it.

'Neither do I,' Hayley muttered. A truth for her. It was impossible to believe that someone like Kate wouldn't have offers every night. She, on the other hand, was too detached to succumb to such craziness.

A twinge of insecurity rode through her, making her stomach tense in an altogether different way. Kate would be used to hot young women under her fingertips. Hayley knew she was in shape, but her body was that of someone who had lived. It had scars and marks of existence. It told her secrets if you knew where to look.

But if Kate was used to something better, something younger and lithe, then she gave no indication that Hayley wasn't up to scratch. With the first layer of clothing removed, she returned to tormenting her with kisses, letting her hands roam up her stomach to cup the soft material of her bra. Hayley took a moment to curse the lack of femininity in her perfectly functional underwear. This hadn't, after all, been on her mind when she had dressed for painting that morning.

As the clasp at the back came undone under Kate's deft hands, she realised it wasn't going to be on long enough to be an issue regardless.

The material hit the floor and Hayley held her breath as Kate's kisses moved from her neck down to her collarbone. With exquisite slowness, her hands cupped her breasts, taking a nip of flesh with her lips at the same moments as she ran the pads of her thumbs over Hayley's swollen nipples.

Hayley's legs trembled as her entire body arched towards Kate. It had been too long. So long since she had felt this turned on it was almost painful. Her hands wrapped into Kate's hair, pulling her in closer with an unrestrained need.

She guided her head down to her right nipple, feeling her body turn molten as Kate flicked it gently with her tongue. Then she took it hungrily into her mouth, sucking and pulling until Hayley began to moan in pleasure.

'Too many clothes,' she muttered, reaching down and tugging at Kate's t-shirt. The pleasure she felt needed to be shared. As much as she craved being at Kate's mercy for hours, she wanted to touch and feel for herself.

Kate took a step back, trailing her hand across Hayley's stomach with teasing slowness. She reached down to the hem of her top and pulled it slowly upwards, revealing inch by inch the tanned hardness of her stomach, glistening in the moonlight.

She pulled the offending material off completely and threw it down on the floor next to Hayley's abandoned clothing. As she reached behind her back to unclasp her bra, Hayley held her breath. Then the straps were sliding down her shoulders, revealing two perfect breasts that told Hayley the arousal she felt was as great as her own.

About to move forward and claim them, she paused when Kate reached for the button of her shorts. She tugged them open, sliding the zip down slowly. As she tucked her fingers into the waistband, Hayley thought she might pass out unless she could make her lungs breathe in again.

Kate slid them down her thighs dragging the material of her underwear with them. Once they reached her knees, she let go, the material of both pooling on the floor around her ankles. She stepped free of them, completely naked, and held out her hand to Hayley as she stepped towards the bed.

For someone who didn't do this often, Kate knew how to give one hell of a strip tease.

Hayley needed no further invitation.

She was kissing Kate again before they reached the bed, Kate tugging frantically at her shorts to remove the final barrier between the two of them. Hayley couldn't think to help her, hands exploring for the first time the softness of the body in front of her. Fingers were hungry for it all; they grazed the softness of Kate's breasts before sliding down her back and down further, pulling the two of them together.

She slid her hands over the smooth expanse of Kate's stomach as her clothing came free and they finally had nothing more than the hot night air between them. Without waiting for permission, she slid her hand lower, through short curls until her fingers found slick and swollen flesh waiting for her.

Kate groaned and threw her head back, exposing her neck to Hayley's mouth and rocked forwards against her hand. It was an old, new feeling, like a memory that she was living for the first time. She slid her hand forward, one finger tentatively finding entrance and Kate gripped her harder, holding onto her for life itself.

Sensing the danger of standing, Hayley slid her hands

free, ignoring Kate's protest and growl of frustration. She guided her down onto the bed pushing her back. She wanted to have complete control. To give Kate the kind of pleasure that she needed.

As she took a nipple in her mouth, her hand reached down, once again seeking the warm space between Kate's thighs. She felt the power and desire rush through her as Kate's legs parted voluntarily, offering herself entirely to Hayley, shameless in the moonlight that covered them both.

Hayley pushed forward with two fingers, testing, stretching, as Kate writhed beneath her hands, pulling away and pushing forwards. Hips moved involuntarily as Hayley brushed the soft nub of nerves with the pad of her thumb. She rolled it back and forth, drunk in the feeling of Kate clenching around her fingers.

Hayley looked up Kate's body to find Kate looking back at her, mouth open in a silent *oh*.

It was the most beautiful thing she had ever seen. Kate's expression was unguarded, her soul as open as her body. Doubts and hesitation clouded Hayley's mind for the briefest of moments, before the thrust of Kate's hips told her not to stop.

Fingers moving in a constant rhythm, Hayley moved her lips down from Kate's breast, kissing across her stomach to form her own constellations. The pattern led to the lowest point and she positioned herself between Kate's thighs, giddy and drunk for the first taste of her.

She nipped and tugged at the soft sensitive skin at the top of Kate's thigh, first one and then the other, working her way higher and closer each time to the place Kate was now begging her to go. She felt hands in her hair, demanding she go higher, that she end the torment. With a swipe of her tongue she moved from where her own fingers plundered flesh to where her thumb had been moments before, pressing the tip of her tongue against the swollen ball of nerves, holding it still in torment as Kate began to shudder beneath her.

The pressure was beginning to build around her fingers and she knew that the combination of hands and mouth had brought Kate close. She moved her tongue back and forth, resisting her own primal urge to go faster. Instead, she kept a steady momentum in time with her fingers, pushing and twisting for that soft ridge of flesh that gave under her fingers and sent Kate over the edge.

She threw her free arm over Kate's hips, holding her in place as she lifted off the bed, her entire body arching into Hayley's mouth and hands. She quivered, vulnerable, beneath her for a few long seconds, drawing out the pleasure that wracked its way through her entire body. Then she dropped to the bed, pleading for Hayley to stop, her senses overloaded beyond the point of sweet torture.

Hayley watched as Kate shuddered and subsided, her body glistening with sweat. The soft sheen that covered her skin made her more beautiful that anything Hayley had ever seen. In her darkest dreams, she had not imagined she would ever feel the power of her own touch bring such a woman to her knees.

Fingers still deep inside, she kissed her way up the body spread before her, tracing the curve of her hip with the tip of her tongue, up between the soft valley of her breasts until her mouth was once again on lips, the sweet salty taste of Kate's body still on her tongue.

She felt Kate's hand slide down to cover her own, pushing her in before pulling her out. 'My turn,' she whispered, turning Hayley's insides molten at the prospect of Kate's fingers inside her. Hands still intertwined, Kate moved between her thighs and Hayley could feel how wet she was, already tense in anticipation.

There was no time to be embarrassed by the obvious extent of her own desire. Kate pushed her onto her back and straddled her thighs. She could see the effects of her own body on Kate's, the skin between her thighs glistening in the moonlight as her legs spread over Hayley's body. At some point Kate's hair had come free and she felt it spread over her like a curtain as Kate bent down to capture her lips once again.

For what felt like hours, but was in reality only minutes, Kate touched and tasted every inch of her skin - every inch other than those few where Hayley needed her to explore deepest. Then, as Hayley thought she was about to go out of her mind, uttering incoherent pleadings for release, Kate's hand slid up her thigh and plunged fingers deep inside; a single thrust that pushed her to the edge of reason, filling her and hollowing her soul out all at once.

Her own words made no sense as they echoed in her ears, begging and demanding, requesting more even as Kate used the weight of her own body to drive her hand deeper inside. The world exploded around Hayley, every muscle and nerve in her body singing as she grabbed and clawed at Kate to pull her in closer. The crescendo stretched out to the edge of her consciousness as it washed over her, the strongest orgasm of her life threatening to blow everything she had ever known apart.

Then Kate was bringing her down, slow movements of fingertips and lips bringing her back to earth. Her body continued to shake at the touch, satiated even as the sight of Kate made her want more.

Hours later, as Kate traced the faded outline of the Celtic knot tattoo on the base of her spine with one hand and spread Hayley's legs wider with her knees, she didn't think her body could take any more pleasure. Then Kate touched her again, a new angle, a different sensation of breasts against her back, as hands plundered and all doubts fled from her mind.

It was only as Kate's deep, even breathing on her neck signalled that sleep should come, that her brain caught up with her body and all they had done. Swollen flesh, a painful reminder of the lines she had crossed and the promises she had broken.

Having never known before, the knowledge she would leave behind in the moonlight would forever be more painful by its absence from now on.

CHAPTER TWO

Kate felt the low rumble of thunder. She cracked one eye to the light and realised it was only in her head. That had been some night.

She forced her breathing to slow so she could listen to the sounds around her. Specifically, for the sound of breathing that would belong to another person.

There was nothing.

Already knowing what she would find, she rolled over. The space next to her was empty, ruffled sheets and a dent in the pillow the only indications that someone else had been there at all.

Damn.

Kate groaned and hid her face in the pillow. It had been far too long since she had spent the night with someone. She never did that. She hadn't lied to Hayley the previous evening just to get her into bed.

It would have been easy, too easy in fact, to leave a trail of one night stands behind her, like a body map of the places she had been to. But that wasn't her style.

It had been close, a few times. Full moon parties when she'd had too much to drink and there was a sense of *what the hell* in the air. When an attractive woman had made it clear they were more than open to the idea of hooking up. Kate knew some female backpackers included a fling with another woman on their list of things to do before they went back home and settled down into the life that was expected of them. A female version of sowing their wild oats. The Americans were the worst, she'd discovered. Those Bible Belt girls who wanted to cross the line far away from home.

She didn't need to prove anything to anyone else and certainly not to herself.

Hayley had been different.

How, she couldn't describe, but from the moment she had emerged from the hostel and seen her standing there, something inside had clicked. As the guy who owned the place had scampered off to make up a room she was fairly confident hadn't been prepared for her arrival, the decision to stay had been made. She'd not expected to find someone like Hayley on this leg of her travels.

She'd stopped looking for someone like Hayley at all.

As they'd talked, she'd seemed distant to begin with. Instead of taking the hint, Kate had found herself more curious than anything else. There had clearly been an attraction there, but Kate could tell Hayley would never make the first move. She was older and Kate had assumed that meant more experienced. If that was the case, she had been hesitant at the start.

Neither of them were hesitating by the end.

This certainly wasn't how she'd expected to start her first day on the island.

Kate pushed herself up on the pillows and looked around. Any sign of Hayley would be a bonus, but she knew it was wishful thinking. She had known from the moment she'd woken up that she was alone and would be until she plucked up the courage to emerge from the room.

She looked around with a sudden rush of fear. Damn, she was such an idiot. Despite the banging head, she dashed out of bed, tearing open the zips on her backpack.

Her laptop was still there. So was her purse with cash and cards.

Kate sat back on her heels, a wave of relief washing through her so strong that she thought she might throw up. Another reason why she didn't have one night stands. She'd heard too many stories about waking up from a night of hot sex with your possessions gone. No money, no passport. It was every backpacker's nightmare, but it never stopped them from taking the risk in the first place. Alcohol, hormones and freedom were a heady mix.

She crawled back to bed. It would be more than the hassle of filling in the police report for her if things got stolen. Without her laptop, without her camera, she was really screwed.

Kate hadn't been entirely honest with Hayley the previous evening. She wasn't just passing through. That was what made the whole thing so much worse. She had no idea how long Hayley was planning to be around, but Kate was likely to outstay her. There would be no quick escape before the two of them ended up bumping into each other on the way to the bathroom. She needed to stay here until her work was done. That would be until she knew enough about the island - one part of it in particular - to write her articles. She was here before any other travel writer. She could break the news of this place. First in, most hits on the website. Big numbers meant more money going into her bank account and even less need to go home and get a soul-sucking job.

Speaking of which, she looked at her watch and realised it was later than she thought. She had spent a few days in London before taking the flight here, but before that, she had been in Cambodia. The jet lag was still wrapping its tentacles around her this morning.

Kate gathered her toiletries bag and towel, poking her head out the door and checking the corridor for signs of life before dashing to the bathroom. Most mornings she enjoyed the social elements of hostel life. People planning their days over breakfast, or listening to tales of the previous day's adventures, were all part of the appeal when she stayed in a communal place. Not that she did that much these days. Since she had built herself a career out of travel, she usually rented small apartments. With the significant cost of living difference between Asia and Europe, she'd decided to downgrade back to a hostel. Pablo's place was the only option and cost as much as her previous apartment that had been part of a complex with its own pool, gym and grocery store.

Yes, Pablo's was definitely a change in style.

She turned on the shower and waited. After a few seconds, a weak spray of water came out. She tested it with her hand. The day was already warm, but she sure as hell didn't need anything that cold on her skin just yet. Turning the tap with the red sticker up full, she prayed that it would produce something hot. The prospect of standing under chilly water wasn't an appealing one, but she had to get the smell of sex off her skin before she saw anyone else.

The thought brought a blush to her face that went a good way towards warming her up properly. Was Hayley still even in the building? They hadn't discussed travel plans. For all Kate knew, that had been Hayley's last night in town and she'd decided to go out with a bang.

No pun intended.

With a low grumble, the pipe work on the wall began to tremble. Kate stared at it in horror, frozen in indecision. Before she could back away, the water pressure jumped with a hiss, bringing with it warm water. She let out a held breath of relief. This was definitely the kind of place she hadn't been to since her earliest travel days.

Once she had washed away the night before and packed her bag for the day, she locked her room and made her way through the dark hallway to the front door. She needed to get breakfast and check out the town that had been in darkness when she'd arrived. Somewhere in the building, she could hear Pablo singing to himself, a Spanish song interspersed with hammering and occasional swearing that needed no translation. Kate contemplated asking him what he knew about Hayley. No, that would be too embarrassing. Besides, just because the two of them had been talking when she'd arrived and throughout dinner didn't mean he really knew anything about her.

Worse, if he had heard them the previous evening, then that was a whole other thing she wasn't ready to face.

She straightened her shoulders. One out-of-character night wasn't something to be ashamed of. She hadn't come here to improve her love life. She had a job to do. It was time to let it go and move on.

#

Three hours later, she stood looking at the skyline, all thoughts of Hayley temporarily forgotten. The sun was hot, but she'd read that at this time of the year, the heat wouldn't tip into ferocious. She was well prepared anyway. A life growing up in Australia followed by travel in the tropics meant water and sunscreen were her daily friends. Her mother had passed along mousey blonde hair and slow-to-tan skin, but after three years of avoiding an office, she had eventually turned a light brown. She remained cautious, especially when she was out in a new place alone like this, but the day had turned out just perfect.

From this vantage point, in the distance she could see the ocean, twinkling its deep blue. Behind her, an interesting formation of rocks had caught her attention and brought her to this spot. It reminded her of a miniature Uluru. Very, very miniature. She pointed her camera and took another shot. Small, but perfectly formed.

Kate checked the screen of her camera to review the picture. It was good, but the hike from Pablo's would be even more amazing at sunrise and sunset. She would come back another day to capture those moments. The world had come to expect a perfect sunset shot in her articles. She couldn't wait to tell everyone about this place. It would surprise her readers, she knew. From the tropics of Asia to the dry heat of Europe, she wasn't sure many of her readers were even aware she had made the change.

Surprising them would keep things fresh. As they lived their lives vicariously through her, she did everything she could to keep it exciting.

She sat down on a rock and pulled a protein bar from her backpack. It was slightly sticky in the heat, and she crinkled her nose at the mess in the wrapper. At least it tasted good, almost like actual chocolate if she pretended hard enough. As she chomped happily, she looked around, her eyes drawn to the bright flowers that were starting to bloom, untamed and unhindered. New signs erected by the regional government protection workers would be useful to the visitors when they began to trickle in, but she didn't need them. *Canarina canariensis*, its flowers like peachy red bells hanging down. She'd done her research before arriving in Spain. Her memory was almost photographic when it came to plants and places.

As she washed the final mouthful down with water, she smiled to herself. This was a good life. She'd made it out of nothing but her own passion. She could travel, she could do the things she loved most. She was free.

She didn't need a relationship to tie her down or hold her back. Not even with an amazing woman like Hayley.

CHAPTER THREE

Hayley was still aching two days after her late night encounter with Kate. As she lifted a crate of beer in the back room, unfamiliar muscles screamed out with pain. She'd thought that running the bar-cafe for years had kept her body in shape. She rarely drank into the profits, so it was all work and movement for her. Lifting crates of beer and soft drinks had kept her arms toned. Mopping the floor after a particularly rowdy night did the same job, although was a far less pleasant way of achieving the same effect.

Making love to Kate had used different muscle groups entirely. It had been a constant reminder ever since and she both loved and hated the feeling. It was a classic battle of body versus mind and she hadn't felt it wage within her for years.

Her brain told her it was a stupid mistake. Regrettable. One she wouldn't make again. Her body, on the other hand, was a reminder that she was human after all. Every woman had needs. Besides, it had been flattering to be wanted by someone young and pretty. No man would be feeling remorse over an encounter like that, so why should she?

She knew why of course, pushing the thought from her head as soon as it appeared.

Stupid mistake or not, she had spent yesterday unable to get Kate off her mind. She had hoped that today would be different. Delivery day didn't really leave a lot of room for thinking at the best of times. Unfortunately, Kate had been on her thoughts more than they had been off. She could be four crates of beer short and she wouldn't have noticed a thing.

In the years of owning the *Segunda Casa* bar, she had never been this distracted by anything. It was her life. A relaxed cafe during the day, it eased into a bar popular with locals once the sun went down. It had been struggling to generate an income when she had visited the small town for the first time. When she saw *Se Vende* above the window, it was both a physical and metaphorical sign. She knew she would buy the place. She had been looking for a home and it was here that she found it.

Hayley had a little experience at serving customers but zero at running a business. In those first few months, she was lucky that hardly anybody had ventured through the doors. It gave her chance to learn the ropes. Learn the language. Become friends with Pablo, who had stuck by her ever since. Once she had convinced him that she really wasn't interested in him and never would be, of course. His pride had smarted for a while, but he'd got over it.

She'd not been looking for friends. That wasn't what

home meant to her. It wasn't a sociable thing. Being alone was a pleasure, not a chore. Pangs of loneliness were pains other people suffered, not her.

Until the other night, a traitorous voice reminded her.

She shut it down and pushed the last crate of beer into its place. She wiped her brow, unsurprised to find the sweat beaded there. The rest of the day would be easier now the most backbreaking work was done.

Back behind the bar, she sent Marco home. Disgraced from the biggest local hotel, hers was the only place he could work. She didn't care that he'd had a fling with one of the customers. She didn't even care that the woman had been on her honeymoon when it happened. Or that they had accidentally been witnessed mid-action by an elderly couple. There was no proof that the old man's heart attack was directly related. Besides, he'd recovered and returned the following season. Other people's relationships were other people's problems and he was an excellent barman. It didn't hurt that he was easy on the eye for half the patronage that came in either, which was what got him into trouble in the first place.

But it was still low season and the afternoon would be slow. She could manage the handful of customers who found their way in until he came back for his main shift at six.

As she waved goodbye to him, he bumped into someone coming through the main doors in the opposite direction. She watched as he did a double take of appreciation before she realised who it was.

Of all the gin joints, she thought wryly to herself.

Kate apologised to Marco in hesitant Spanish before

walking the rest of the way into the bar. Hayley took advantage of the few seconds she had before Kate's eyes adjusted to the light. Part of her had hoped that without the aid of beer goggles, Kate was average and unattractive. It would be less flattering to her ego, but easier to live with in the long term. Instead, she was exactly as Hayley remembered.

Her memory ran wild uncontrollably for a second with *all* the ways she did remember her and Hayley felt the colour flood her cheeks before there was anything she could do to stop it. What the hell was she still doing here?

Apparently, Kate was thinking the same thing. Hayley saw the silent 'oh!' of surprise when she was finally spotted in her hiding place behind the wooden counter that was acting as a shield. She was gripping it tightly. There was no way out now unless Kate turned round on her heels and walked out of the bar.

Instead, she stepped forwards. Of course she did. Why did Hayley think she would be lucky enough to have an easy life? Some things never changed.

'Hey there,' said Kate, walking up to the bar, a huge grin on her face. Hayley found herself smiling in response, despite her best intentions to remain purely professional. She was here to provide the girl with a refreshing drink, nothing else.

'Hi.' Smooth.

'This looks like a sweet gig. How did you land this one?'

'A sweet gig?' Hayley repeated slowly. What did that mean?

'Working behind the bar. I'd read they only really

employ locals around here.'

'They do.'

'You must be as charming to everyone else as you were to me then.' Kate leaned her elbows on the bar and Hayley could feel herself begin to soften.

'I didn't really have to be.' The only person she'd had to convince to give her this *sweet gig* was herself. 'I didn't think you'd still be around.'

'You sound disappointed to see me.'

'No.' Quickly. Too quickly. Hayley's grip on the bar tightened again. 'I just meant don't backpackers, you know, travel? Backpack? Isn't that the point? To keep moving?'

'I'm not exactly a backpacker.'

'You're not?' now Hayley was genuinely confused. Why would you stay at Pablo's place if you weren't a backpacker in need of a cheap place to stay? There were plenty of hotels in the area that could guarantee hot water and clean towels. She wasn't sure he had either properly sorted yet.

'No, I do. I mean, I travel. A lot. I started as a backpacker, I guess. It's hard to explain.'

'Try me.' Despite her promises to herself, she wanted to know more about the woman who knew the constellations and how to trace them with her fingers.

'I write about where I travel. Blogs, articles, review sites, that kind of thing. I make enough money to keep going. I could never stay in one place for long.' It was a throwaway line, but one that caused a swift, temporary ache in Hayley's chest. Any fleeting hopes of a beautiful romance, hopes that she knew she shouldn't allow herself to have in the first place, died. Kate couldn't settle, she wouldn't travel. It was hardly a perfect match. It sounded like an interesting life.

For someone else to live.

'That sounds like a lot of fun.' Hayley tried not to choke on the disappointment.

'It is. I can't imagine living my life any other way now. Don't get me wrong, it's not always easy. I've been down to my last few dollars more than once. But I'm not proud. If it means working in a bar sometimes like this then I'll do it. What? What did I say?' Kate was surprised by the smirk Hayley couldn't help but show. She obviously thought that she was slumming it by being here. 'I'm not saying I'm looking for something right now. Don't worry, I'm not going to try to take your job away.'

'Glad to hear it.'

'And I'm not going to ask you to have a word with the boss for me either. I'm good for now.'

'Oh, I'm not sure you'd like her anyway.' Hayley shook her head in mock seriousness.

'Really? Why, what's she like?'

'Real slave driver. About so high,' Hayley raised her hand level with the top of her own head. It was just too much fun not to tease Kate a little. 'Hair this sort of colour,' she wiggled the ends of her own between the tips of her fingers. 'She does offer drinks on the house sometimes, if you're in a bar and looking for that kind of thing.'

Hayley popped the top off a bottle and placed it on the wooden counter in front of Kate. It was hard not to laugh as her expressions changed with her thought process, moving quickly from interested to confused to understanding. 'Wait, are you saying what I think you're saying?'

'Well that depends on what you think I'm saying.'

'You don't just work here? You manage the place?' Kate looked over her shoulder and around the bar, as if waiting for someone to jump out and shout *surprise!*

'Not quite. I own the place. This is my bar.'

'Then...' Kate was clearly having difficulty processing a turn of events. 'The other night,' she blurted.

'I'm sorry.' She was. For more than just this, but there was no point telling Kate that either.

'Why didn't you say something?'

'It didn't come up. I'm sorry. I didn't lie. I just thought there was no need to mention it.' Now she said the words aloud, it sounded like a weak excuse.

'So you're not staying there?'

'At Pablo's? No way. I mean,' she recovered hastily, 'it's going to be an amazing place and it has a lovely view, but it would be too far for me to travel each day.'

'You're right about going to be. Right now, it's no palace.'

'It's his first time trying something like this. And his heart is in the right place. Pablo is a lovely guy.'

'He is very sweet.'

'He's one of my best friends. That was why I was there when you arrived. I'd been helping him on my day off to finish up the place. Then we got talking and, well, one thing led to another. I didn't think I'd see you again.'

'Is that why you left without saying goodbye?' Ouch.

'I had to get back here. I figured you probably wouldn't want to see me again anyway.'

'I don't know if that's some kind of an insult.'

'I don't mean for it to be, I promise. I just thought there was no point dragging out an embarrassing morning after. Not if you would be off again straight away. I was trying to make it easier for both of us.'

'You still should have said goodbye.'

'I know. You can have another drink on the house if it helps?'

'It's a start. But you're wrong.'

'About?'

'Me. Two things. I'm not into one night stands and I'm not going anywhere. Not for a couple of weeks at least. I have some work to do here. So I'll be staying awhile.'

'Oh.' Hayley didn't know how to handle the sudden war of emotions. The thought that she could see Kate again rushed up inside her first, followed by the fear that she would have to. That whatever she had been feeling since the moment she first saw her was not going to go away any time soon. Then regret followed, swift on the heels of the others, chasing them away. What Kate was telling her changed nothing. She still couldn't - shouldn't - go there.

'Which means I'd like to see you again.' Kate gave her a huge smile. As if it was as simple as saying it out loud.

'I don't think that's a good idea.' Hayley forced the words out but they sounded unconvincing to her own ears.

'You don't?' Kate frowned. 'I thought we were good together.'

'We were. I'm sorry. I'm really not looking for a relationship right now. Or even a casual fling. I don't really do them, despite the terrible first impression you have of me.'

'Didn't you hear me earlier? I don't do them either. I know you think we're all doing that kind of thing, travelling the world, partying, sleeping around, but I'm not.'

'Then that's the one thing we agree on. Everything else, we're on different pages. Trust me. It's not going to happen.'

'Surely the fact we both did something so unlike our normal selves to be together means something? Don't I get a say in this?'

'No. I'm sorry. God, I feel like I'm apologising a lot. I wish things were different, but they're not.' Hayley knew she was doing a bad job of explaining things. But how could she, really, without telling Kate everything?

The door opened and an elderly couple walked in, over-brown wrinkled skin glistening in the sunlight that filtered in from outside. Regulars. Hayley breathed a sigh of relief. It would end the conversation before she could put her foot in it any more than she already had. 'I need to serve these people.'

'That's okay, I'll go. See you around Hayley.' She put the half-finished bottle back down on the bar.

'Bye.'

Hayley waited until Kate had left before gently banging her head against the surface of the bar. That couldn't have gone any worse if she'd tried. 'Your coffees will be right up,' she called out to the couple who were getting comfortable at their usual table. Three months every year they were here and they hadn't had anything different yet.

That was her life. Her routine. She wasn't like Kate, full

of youth and adventure. She was finally settled.

She intended to stay that way.

So why did she feel like she had just missed the first chance for happiness she'd had since she'd arrived here all those years ago?

CHAPTER FOUR

This, Kate knew, was the downside of staying in hostels, as she turned the volume up one more time. Even the noise-cancelling headphones couldn't drown out the sound of Pablo's jackhammer. Building work was most definitely ongoing.

He was still being sweet about it. He'd spoken to her the previous evening and apologised profusely, almost with comedic sincerity, that the following two days he would be doing some more building works on the hostel. There would be noise, but he would not start until 9am. That, apparently, was a compromise on his part.

Not that the early start mattered to her as she had no intention of repeating her first night of drinking and socialising, with its corresponding next day hangover. Not unless Hayley made another surprise appearance at least. No, it was the inconvenience of it all. She had a video she needed to edit and upload. Her website desperately needed some new material. Without it, money would quickly stop coming in. Going anywhere other than Pablo's would mean forking out more cash right now.

She had been internally debating this catch-22, when Pablo had offered her next week's accommodation at a fifty per cent reduction from the advertised rate. That had sealed the deal in her mind. She simply couldn't justify paying at least five times that just to stay at one of the nearby hotels. Kate might be still be struggling to convert Euros, but she could still spot a good deal when she saw one.

Despite Pablo's bargain rates, this morning she was beginning to regret the decision. She re-read the first outline of her blog post and decided she would have to trash everything apart from the last paragraph. These were not the productive surroundings she had grown used to.

She put the laptop down on the bed next to her. At least she was warm again after the warm water had stopped mid-shower that morning. From the moment she'd tentatively put her body underneath, she had been waiting for it. Like some self-fulfilling prophecy, it waited until the most inconvenient moment to hit her with an icy blast before turning to a dribble. The pipes continued to rumble, but nothing more came out. She was going to have to come up with a Plan B. Or C at this point. Anything that wasn't another eight hours at *Casa Pablo*.

A thought struck her and she pushed it away for only a second before letting it back in. She felt the excitement bubble in her stomach. Building work was a good reason to do something she wanted to do anyway. She jumped up and left the room, easily finding Pablo by following the noise until it changed from excruciating to unbearable.

'Hey there Pablo.'

'*Hola*. The noise? It is too much?'

'*Sí*,' she shrugged. There was no point lying. 'Can I ask a question?'

'Of course.'

'Hayley's bar. In town.'

'*Sí*, I know the bar. Hayley does sangria the best in the world. You should try.'

'Thanks for the tip. Do you know if she has wifi?'

'Wifi?'

'I need it. To work.'

'There is wifi here.'

'I know.' Today the wifi was about the only thing still functioning. 'But I need wifi and some quiet. To write.' She mimicked typing on the keypad.

'Ah. I see,' he gave her a grin. 'The bar has wifi. And today, it also has Hayley.'

'I just need the wifi.'

'Of course.' He nodded and she could tell that regardless of the language barrier, he could read her like a book. Kate wasn't prone to caring about what people thought of her, but underneath her tan, she could feel herself begin to blush.

'Thanks.' She turned around and made a hasty exit before she could say anything else to incriminate herself, but she still heard Pablo's soft chuckle before she was out of earshot.

She really did need the wifi. But if there were some added benefits, then she wasn't going to complain.

#

The tables outside the bar were full of tourists taking in

the view and basking their bodies in the sunlight. Most of them were already an unhealthy shade of pink and Kate shook her head, a lifetime of being warned about the long-term damage of too much sunlight now seared into her brain.

Not that she would be able to work outside. She needed somewhere cool and dark and that meant inside.

With a good view of the bar, she grinned. Decision made, there was no point feeling guilty about it. Just walking down from the hostel, she could feel her mood getting lighter and the small thrill of seeing Hayley again frothing in her stomach. Despite the denials, she knew the connection between them was different. Special somehow. Before the excitement could take hold and turn the grin from friendly to maniacal, she pushed through the door and into the bar.

It was busier in here too, with those taking shelter from the sun. A surprising number were already drinking beer, but she was strictly a coffee before 5pm kind of girl. As she looked up and saw Hayley looking back at her, she knew she would be staying sober right to the end, no matter what time. Her mouth couldn't be trusted not to say the thoughts that were running through her mind if alcohol was thrown into the mix.

She forced her feet forwards. Standing there like an idiot wasn't going to win over someone who was clearly reluctant to pick up where they left off. Kate had a distinct impression the age gap bothered Hayley in the cold light of day. Standing there blushing like a teenager would do nothing to disabuse her of that notion. She decided to hit her with the full on Aussie charm.

'G'day.'

'*Hola.*' A small smile played on Hayley's lips and Kate knew her plan had worked.

'I thought I'd pay you a visit. Pablo's place is a building site today.'

'Stopping you from sleeping in huh?'

'Sleeping in isn't my thing. Having a decent shower and a quiet place to work is.'

'I can't guarantee quiet here.'

'Trust me, compared to up there, this place is like a temple. He told me you have wifi?'

'I do. You need a password.'

'And what do I need to do to get that password?'

'You have to ask a member of staff and buy something from the bar.'

'In that case, please can I get a flat white and the wifi password?'

'A flat white? Seriously?'

'Yes.'

'You don't come to Spain and order a flat white. A cafe latte or even a cappuccino, but not a flat white.'

'Oh.' Kate eyes flicked around for a menu.

'I can make you a flat white. But don't tell anyone. I'm a barwoman, not a barista catering to coffee-based beverages from all around the globe. Take a seat and I'll bring it over to you.'

'And the wifi password?'

'I'll bring that too.'

'Thanks.'

Kate looked around the room at table options and selected one near the far wall. It wasn't what most people would consider a prime location, but she knew it was perfect. No one behind her, so she didn't have to feel self-conscious about what she was working on. More importantly, it gave her an unobstructed view of the bar.

She had been on the lookout for inspiration. Right now, Hayley was it.

By the time she was set up, Hayley came over with her drink. 'One flat white.'

'Thanks.'

'Do you still need the wifi password?'

'Yup.'

'Password. All lower case.' Hayley gave her a grin and walked off.

'You make people buy a drink for that?' Kate called after her.

'Be grateful I didn't make you order food,' Hayley shot back and Kate couldn't stop the chuckle. It wasn't even funny. Whatever it was that she found attractive about Hayley, she had it bad.

She typed in the password and waited for it to connect. It wasn't exactly one of the co-working spaces she had been used to in Thailand, but it was light-years away from the experience she was having at Pablo's.

The coffee was better too, she thought, appreciating the taste from the very first sip. Tea and coffee came free with the hostel kitchen, a nice touch, but it was the supermarket's own basic variety. Enough to give her what she needed to get out of bed each morning, but hardly a taste sensation in her mouth.

Unlike Hayley, a childish voice in the back of her mind giggled.

No, nothing was quite like Hayley. She watched from over the top of her screen as the object of her sudden passions moved behind the bar with fluid ease. She was completely at home there. Kate wondered how many years it had been since she had bought the place. She stored the question away for later conversation.

There would be later conversation, she would make sure of that.

Right now, she needed to focus, she reminded herself. The longer it took to write the articles, the longer she would have to work. Here. No wonder she was dragging her feet. No article, no pay, she also reminded herself. And no pay meant no money for coffee. If that was the minimum entry requirement to be around Hayley for a few hours, then she would have to get moving.

Thirty minutes later the coffee was gone, but the second attempt at writing was also complete. Kate skimmed over the paragraphs. Yes, they were much better than the first draft. Far from perfect, but the bar had been subtly quiet enough to allow her to concentrate around the conversations going on. Over the years, she had grown used to tuning out the voices of others. Power tools were a different matter.

'What are you doing?' Hayley's voice made Kate jump. The moment she'd stopped paying attention was the moment she made her move. 'That's a lot of time on Facebook.'

'Ha ha, very funny. I'm writing an article. For my website.'

'You must take it very seriously if you're in here on a nice sunny day when you could be at the beach instead.'

'There'll be time for the beach. It's there any day. This,' she gestured at the screen, 'needs to appear on my site tomorrow.'

'Or what?'

'Or I won't get paid.'

'Oh.' Hayley didn't seem to believe her.

'I wasn't trying to fool you when I said I wasn't really a backpacker, you know. This is my job. It might not be behind a bar or sitting in an office, but it's my career. I have to take it seriously.'

'What on earth is there to write about here? This is the least exciting town I know.' She leant forward and lowered her voice, giving Kate a view of her cleavage in the process. 'I mean, have you looked at the clientele? Most of them are old enough to have a heart attack if anything interesting actually happened.'

'You would be surprised.'

'You'd better not be writing about this place.' There was a smile on Hayley's lips but something about her tone told Kate she was being serious. Stern, almost icy. It wasn't like people to pass up free marketing. Hayley must know that Kate liked her enough that she'd only write a favourable review? It didn't make sense that as a bar owner she wouldn't want a boost in the Tripadvisor rankings. Kate stored the nugget of information away for later. She'd already worked out that Hayley wasn't going to be pushed into talking about anything she didn't want to.

'No, I'm not writing about the bar. I might ask Pablo if I can write about the hostel though. Not yet, but when I leave. Right now, I'm not sure even the most skilfully worded article could convince people it was paradise if they saw any photos. He keeps promising that it's nearly done. When it is, I think it will be popular with a lot of people.'

'I still don't know why young people would want to come here on their way to anywhere.'

'Young people? Are you including yourself in that?' Kate couldn't help but take a soft jibe. She needed to know if it was part of the reason why Hayley seemed intent on pushing her away.

'In comparison to this lot? I would have to. In comparison to a bunch of backpackers, then I'm sure they'd see it the other way around.'

'Well one day soon I'll surprise you.'

'Oh really?' Hayley seemed amused that Kate would know more than she did.

'How long have you been here?'

'Twelve years.' It rolled off the tongue, as if Hayley had been crossing the days off the calendar. Everything this woman said made her seem more and more interesting.

'Long enough that you've stopped seeing the things in front of you. It's completely normal. We all become immune to the place we stay in for a long time.'

'Is that why you keep moving?'

'One of the reasons. I love waking up to something I've never seen before. Especially when the culture is so different. I love that life can continue to be so exciting.'

'Are you calling my life here dull?'

'Now you're just putting words into my mouth.' Kate kept smiling. There was a chance she had offended but she needed to push her way through it if she had. 'But one day I'll show you everything with a fresh pair of eyes.'

'I have to go.' Hayley looked up as another elderly couple came through the door. Was that all it was? Kate thought she'd leapt at the excuse to escape. Was a day out together really such a bad prospect? It had been such a long time since Kate had been in a relationship with anyone, but she could spot commitment issues a mile off. Hayley definitely had those and then some.

She watched as Hayley made her way back around the bar to get her small notebook. She glanced back at Kate as she walked over to the table where the couple were settling themselves in. Then it was all professional, all cheery service, as if Kate wasn't there at all. As if they'd not had a conversation that had been steadily working its way towards them going on a date together.

A day date, but a date nonetheless. She just needed to make sure Hayley didn't realise it.

#

An hour later and she was doing the final checks on her article when a plate appeared on the table next to her. She'd been so engrossed she hadn't noticed the time tick by. The plate was joined by another flat white and she grinned in appreciation. 'What's this?'

'You looked like you were working so hard I thought you might forget to eat.'

'Unlikely,' Kate looked at her watch. It was indeed later than she thought. 'Or apparently not. Thank you.'

'It's nothing much. Just a little bit of tapas. The lunch service is beginning, so it was nothing to give you a little bit extra. Shit, you're not a vegetarian are you? I can't remember what you ate from Pablo's barbecue.'

'No. You're safe.'

'Good. There are *Albóndigas*, *Chorizo al vino*, *Tortilla de patatas* and *Croquetas de jamón*. Oh, and I thought you might like another coffee. I can get you some water as well if you want?'

'You really didn't have to do this. It all looks delicious.'

'Pablo would tell me it wasn't authentic, but it's as close as you're going to get in a bar run by an ex Englishwoman.'

'How much do I owe you?'

'It's on the house.'

'That doesn't seem fair.'

'See it as a thank you for bringing the average age down by a few decades. It's made me feel a little less alone here today.'

'In that case, you'll definitely have to let me return the favour some time. You've shown me your life, so you'll have to let me show you mine. You'll enjoy it, I promise. No pressure,' she hastily added when she saw that look of refusal beginning to show in Hayley's eyes. 'Think about it. I'll be around for a while. There's time.'

'We'll see.' It was the closest thing to a compromise that Kate could hope for. 'I'd better get back to it. Just shout if you need anything else.'

'Will do. And thank you. I mean it.' Kate watched as Hayley walked away again, stopping to chat to another couple she clearly knew. The woman made no sense. How could she go from frosty as hell one moment and bringing her free food the next? Not that Kate was ever going to complain about free food. She stuck her fork in the *Albóndigas* and put a piece in her mouth. Hayley might have downplayed the authenticity of the food, but it still tasted amazing. The meatball dissolved on her tongue, filling her mouth with the flavour of ground beef and fresh tomatoes. Despite her extensive travels, Kate wasn't much of a foodie. Certainly not in comparison to some of the people she had met along the way, who seemed to live for the chance to try a new dish every day. For Kate, good food was just an added bonus.

Even so, as she tried a bit of *Chorizo al vino* next, she knew that this was worth it. No wonder the bar had so many regular customers. This was the kind of food you came back for.

Which was a real waste, given that Hayley had seemed anti-marketing. Perhaps she thought an influx of new customers seeking it out as part of their holiday experience would destroy the vibe. She could understand that. There were plenty of places she knew of that had been ruined by a viral internet campaign. With more custom than they could handle, quality suffered. They'd withered and died in the end. There was no point in burning too brightly to sustain the flame. Perhaps Hayley had been through something like that already. After all, if she'd kept the place running for this long, she must know more about business than Kate did, running her little solo venture from her laptop and backpack.

The thought reminded her once again that she should be working, not spending her time agonising over the inner thoughts of a woman she'd spent one night with. It didn't matter that it was the most amazing night she could remember. Hayley had made it very clear that it wouldn't happen again.

But Hayley had also brought her tapas when she could

just as easily have spent the morning ignoring her. If there was even the slightest crack between her words and how she really felt, then Kate knew that there could be a chance. All she had to do was to take it.

She popped another piece of chorizo into her mouth and went back to work, letting the thought settle in her brain. Hayley was too skittish to say yes to anything too obvious. Which meant that Kate needed to become her friend first.

An email alert pinged on the screen in front of her. As she opened it, her brain was already hatching a plan to see Hayley again.

CHAPTER FIVE

Changeover day at the two big hotels just along the coast was always Hayley's favourite day. She had to be the only business owner in the town who enjoyed the evenings when it was quiet. The local economy had taken a hit over recent years when several of the hotels had swapped to become all-inclusive resorts. With all the food and drink they could handle on site, fewer people ventured down into the town. A handful of businesses had closed. Many more were barely hanging on.

She didn't have a family to support and she had money in the bank to get her through the lean times. If she could break even most of the year and turn a profit in high season, then that was good enough for her. Besides, she had resisted turning it into a British bar. Now she had been here for long enough that on many evenings, such as this one, it was mainly locals who filled her tables. It was just the right amount of work for Marco to be able to handle himself most of the time. The locals expected slow and relaxed service. Here, they sometimes got it in spades.

'What are you thinking eh?' Pablo asked and she realised she had drifted off.

'I was just thinking about this place.'

'You are doing well, yes?' Pablo looked around the bar, spotted someone he knew and waved. 'Is everything ok?'

'Yes, everything's fine. What about you? How is the hostel coming along?'

'Every day, a new job. The walls, the ceiling, the pipes, the heating. One thing then the next thing and I am but a man on my own.'

'I'm sure you're doing fine.'

'But perhaps, with a little more help, I could do better?' he grinned at her. Typical Pablo, always out for something. She resisted the urge to reach over the bar and punch him on the shoulder.

'You decided to do this thing. I warned you to get everything finished before you started allowing people to stay.'

'But they are paying me money!'

'Which you're giving back to them in free food because you feel so bad about the mess. I may not understand business like the Hotel Vista Mar, but I know enough to know you won't make any profits that way.'

'The Hotel Vista Mar,' Pablo spat, 'does not understand the needs of the everyday man.'

'Oh dear lord, here we go,' Hayley muttered.

'Only the rich can afford to stay at the Hotel Vista Mar. What about those who wish to see our beautiful ocean? The ones who want to eat our local food? See our local culture? The ones who are like me, just a poor boy, from a poor family?'

'Have you been listening to British radio again by any chance?'

'That is not the point,' he grinned. 'The Hotel Vista Mar, it does not offer any of that. The people stay there and they just lie in the sun all day, eating burgers and drinking cheap Irish Cream. That is not *Español*. That is their culture. But with the sun.'

'I hate to break it to you, but that is exactly what most people up there want from a holiday.'

'Then they are not welcome at Pablo's,' he said defiantly, pounding his fist on the bar. True to form, he had somehow made this a victory for his argument. Hayley couldn't help but laugh.

'So they don't want you and you don't want them. But you still need to get the people who do want to be there to pay you. It's going to be great when it's done, but you have to be careful. A few bad reviews and it will be all over before you get the chance to show them how amazing it could be.'

'Exactly. Which is why I need some extra help to move things along. Think how much faster it could be with two sets of hands.'

'I can think of several pairs of hands who could help you. People with actual building skills. People like your brother, for instance. Why don't you ask them?'

'Because they would expect to be paid.'

'I'd quite like to be paid.'

'No, you would not. The changing of money across hands would not be the act of friendship. I would not risk our friendship for something as meaningless as money.'

'You're quite the poet Pablo. For a cheap bastard.'

'Thank you.'

'I'm not sure it was really a compliment.' She poured him another glass of beer. 'Besides, I could call in your tab and take the summer off.'

'Money ruins friendship, no talking about it,' he wagged his finger in admonishment and took the beer anyway. 'Besides, I can offer you something better than money in exchange for your help.'

'And what is that exactly?'

'One of my customers,' he gave a huge grin.

'Jesus, Pablo, you sound like a pimp. I didn't realise you were planning on running that kind of place.'

'What is this pimp mean?'

'Never mind. I'm going to pretend I don't know what you're talking about.'

'She has paid for another two weeks already. Plenty of chance for you to see her. You could paint.'

'I'm not going to do your dirty work, for free I might add, just so I can see someone who happens to be staying there. That makes me feel creepy.'

'I think she likes you too.'

'Pablo, just let it go.' He was teasing her now and that was fine, but she knew what he was like when he got his mind stuck on something. He was like a dog with a bone. Still, her heart leapt a little at the knowledge that Kate would be around for at least another two weeks. That meant there was a good chance that she would see her again.

She closed her eyes and mentally chastised herself. This was exactly what she had told herself she wouldn't do. She was not going to get involved with anyone. More importantly, not someone like Kate. There were too many reasons why she shouldn't and she was getting sick of reminding herself of them.

Was this what it felt like? Compulsive behaviour? She'd spent her adult life trying to outrun the thought she might lose control of her feelings, her sanity, one day. Was this just the start of it, some old familiar pattern she had somehow inherited? Passed down through her genes? It made her sick just to think about it.

'But it is not right for me to paint the ladies bathroom, no?'

'What?' Hayley realised she had stopped listening again. Sometimes the ghosts in her head talked louder than the real voices in the room.

'The ladies bathroom. It needs to be given its final paint. This is not a job for a man. I do not want to be in there if the ladies, they need to use it. You are a lady. You could help. Just this one small job.'

'Small job?'

'Maybe both ladies bathrooms?'

'There's a second one?'

'It's a big place,' he shrugged. 'Two bathrooms. You would be helping out a friend. What else would you do on your day off? Be alone, or spend it with me?'

'But you've just said you won't be there.' Trying to argue with the man was like being a Kafka character sometimes.

'I will be there after. For the food. The drinks. I will show you my best hospitality.'

'I'm sure you will.' Despite her earlier protests, it was

tempting. He'd hit a nerve too; she never did anything on her day off. She usually stayed above the bar in her apartment, close at hand, in case Marco needed her for anything. He seldom did these days and nothing that couldn't be dealt with via phone rather than in person.

She'd enjoyed being with Pablo and working on the hostel. It had been a long time since she'd had a project she could sink her teeth into. She knew the running of the bar by heart now, small engrained habits that allowed her to move through her day without problems or stress. But that was not the same as having a new challenge to get stuck into. Pablo was right about that. She could see why he went from project to project, seeking out a never-ending source of stimuli.

'Please?' it was quiet this time. Some of the bravado was gone. Hayley could see that behind the brash exterior, Pablo was starting to get worried. He knew she was right. Keeping the guests sweet with free food would work when it was a small number of backpackers with no cash and low expectations, but not everyone would be that way. Someone travelling on the bank of mom and dad or with their trust fund would expect the rooms to be finished, even if they were basic. It would only take someone with a malicious streak to completely tank the venture.

'Okay. I'll help. But only because you really need it.'

'Tomorrow?' At her acquiescence, Pablo brightened again.

'I thought you wanted me to do it on my day off, not take an actual day off just to help you.'

'Marco is a good boy. He can handle it. Besides, tomorrow will be quiet here. You work too hard. You deserve a break.'

'Working for you is damn harder than working for myself.'

'But the view is so much better, yes?' he wiggled his eyebrows and she knew he was referring to Kate again.

'I am only helping you because you are my friend. Nothing else.'

'If you say so.'

'Do you want my help or not?'

'*Si, si*.' He raised his hands in surrender. 'I want your help. I will say nothing else.'

'Good. Hey Marco,' she waved to get his attention at the other end of the bar. 'Do you want to do a full day tomorrow? Caterina will be in to help with the evening shift.'

'*Si*.' Marco went back to work without further discussion. It was a rare occasion he'd ever say no.

'Thanks.' She turned back to Pablo and ignored the smug grin on his face. 'I'll be up there in the morning. And you'd better not surprise me with any other jobs that need doing. Ladies bathrooms only. Nothing else.'

'Of course. I am a man of my word.'

'You are a man of many words, that's what always gets you into trouble.'

'I am wounded.' He clasped his chest with one hand whilst simultaneously holding out his beer glass for a refill with the other.

'One more. Then I'm cutting you off.'

'That is good. I have a very big day too tomorrow.'

'Dare I ask what you'll be doing while I paint your bathrooms?'

'I will be changing the hot water tank.'

'Have you ever done that before?'

'No.'

'Have you ever *seen* one done before?'

'No. But Javier explained to me. It sounds simple.'

'I'm glad you trust Javier.' Pablo's younger brother had a reputation in the old town. He'd been the reason she and Pablo had met. Pablo had been clearing up after another one of Javier's jobs had gone wrong. In her cellar. He had assured her he would be able to do the repair she needed and new to the town, she'd had no choice but to trust him. No one else was available and the job had been urgent. He had, of course, made it worse, then called his older brother to help him out.

She loved Pablo, but couldn't deny that he was blind to the failings of other people. And himself, most of the time. But he was also right; it all worked out in the end. It was a way of life and community that had taken her the better part of a decade to get used to.

'Javier has done this before. He will help if I need.' Pablo accepted the topped up glass of beer with a smile. 'Besides, you are good. It has instruction book. Ladies are good at reading those.'

'I'll ignore your rampant sexism for now.' Hayley knew it wasn't a battle worth fighting after years of trying. It was hard to even know if he was teasing her or not. 'I'll be up there in the morning at nine.'

'Why so late?'

'Because I will be working tonight for a few hours after you leave. I might be willing to help you, but I'm not going to do it on three hours sleep. I'll be there at nine. Take it or leave it.'

'Nine it is.'

'Good.'

'Besides, your friend gets up at eight. I am sure she will be please to see you when she is eating her breakfast.'

'I have the legal right to throw you out of here, you know that?'

'And lose my custom? You would not do that.'

'Do you need me to check your tab before I do?'

'Perhaps not. Hey, did I tell you about my sister Margarite?' With that, Pablo skilfully changed the subject. The topic of Kate was laid to rest for the evening, even if the conversation carried on in Hayley's mind until her eyes finally closed and she drifted to sleep that night.

CHAPTER SIX

Kate closed her eyes, trying to block out the sound of conversation as she stabbed at her muesli. The two Swedish girls were doing her head in. There was no other way of describing it. They gibbered non-stop with uncontrolled enthusiasm and she didn't have the foggiest what they were talking about. She'd learned enough Thai to get by and was picking up Spanish now she was here, but she had no concept at all of Swedish. Other than being of use if she decided to take a trip to IKEA, she could see no reason for learning it either.

The two of them had talked late into the night, which was one of the reasons for her grumpiness that morning. Her trusty earplugs had somehow worked their way free around 2am and it was at that point a piercing giggle woke her up.

For a few seconds, she had been disoriented. Her heart pounded, trying to place the sound that had woke her, the fear of an intruder sending her into panic mode. As her eyes adjusted to the dark and she became aware of her surroundings, the laughter came again, shrill even through the thick walls. The adrenalin subsided, leaving a shaky fury in its wake. She had finally managed to get back to sleep, but the bad mood had been hard to dispel when she woke up.

It wasn't their fault, she knew. They were here on a normal, backpacking experience. The whole point was to travel and have fun without a care in the world. She was the one who was different. She'd grown used to living in a different way, that was all. A little bit older, a little bit wiser.

It didn't help that she had a busy day planned. A day when she would have to use her brain. A brain that worked best when it had experienced a good night's sleep. So, it was either murder Celia and Anneka, or find a different place to be for the day. She was briefly torn between the two, but decided that the hard rock surrounding the hostel would make it impossible to bury bodies.

She could always borrow Pablo's jackhammer...

Kate let the thought trail off before her brain could complete its murderous plan. Going somewhere else for the day was better than the alternative. She could go to Hayley's bar. Would that be too obvious? She was determined not to push things. But it really was better for her sanity. She could almost hear Hayley's voice in her head and it was like sweet music compared to the babble that was surrounding her.

No, wait. That actually was Hayley's voice.

Kate snapped out of her reverie, spoon halfway

towards her mouth. She strained her ears. Yes, that was definitely Hayley. The noise of the corridor leading from the (allegedly soon to be finished) reception to the kitchen area always echoed. What the hell was she doing here?

Before she could answer her own question, Hayley walked into the room, her eyes finding Kate's own with uncanny accuracy. Kate realised she was doing her best mannequin impression and hovered for a few seconds longer, unable to determine if putting the spoon down or actually eating the contents was the best course of action. She opted for the former. 'Hi.'

'Morning. Don't let me interrupt you.'

'That's okay.' She paused. Pablo stood behind Hayley grinning like an idiot. Kate had a moment of panic. The two of them were friends. Had Hayley said anything about her? About what they had done together than night? 'I was done anyway.'

'I thought I'd just grab myself a coffee. I can wait until you're finished though?'

'No, really. Go ahead.'

'I will leave you,' said Pablo with another slightly crazed grin before he dashed back out into the hallway.

'Is he always like this?' Kate asked, picking up her bowl and crossing the kitchen. When Hayley joined her at the counter she caught a hint of her perfume and tried not to inhale. It flooded her memories with the soft scent. Citrus, with a hint of something else.

'He has his moments. Once he gets his mind set on something, I usually have to give up persuading him otherwise.' She picked up a cup from the draining board and checked it suspiciously before deciding it was clean enough to risk. 'Which is how I ended up here again.'

'You're not here just for the coffee?' Kate smiled as Hayley picked up the jar.

'Definitely not. I nearly brought my own just in case. You don't have a secret stash in your room by any chance?'

'I'm afraid not.'

'Shame. This will have to do.'

'So if it's not for the coffee, then why are you here? Pablo said last night he was going to be working again all day.'

'He is. And you're looking at his faithful assistant.'

'Oh.' Kate's mind began to whirr. Only minutes earlier she had been looking forward to packing up her stuff and getting the hell out of there. Now, perhaps, this could change her mind. 'What does he need you to do?'

'I have been promised it is nothing more than painting the female bathrooms. Two at the most. Of course, this is Pablo, so it could turn into just about anything.' Hayley poured boiling water into her cup and wrinkled her nose in distaste at the dirty brown drink. Kate thought it was cute. Get a grip, she told herself.

'Painting doesn't sound so bad. I'm sure he could come up with much worse.'

'Oh, he definitely could.' Hayley turned around and leaned back against the counter, taking a first tentative sip of her drink. 'This is not good. Seriously, next time I'll bring my own. So what are your plans for the day? Heading out anywhere nice?'

'Um,' Kate hesitated, torn between what she wanted to do and what she knew she should do. 'I've not really got any plans,' she lied. It sounded convincing, at least to her own ears. As long as they didn't make eye contact Hayley might believe her. The next words were out of her mouth before her brain had the chance to censor her. 'I could help you with the painting if you want?'

'I hardly think that's fair. You're paying to stay here, not paying to work here.'

'It's of benefit to me too. I have to use those bathrooms, remember?'

'I'm still not sure that's how it works.'

'I'll make you a deal. If I get bored, I'll head out and do my own thing. But right now, painting sounds better than sitting around doing nothing.'

'I thought you did a lot of work from your laptop?'

'Day off.' The lies were coming thick and fast. It surprised her how easy it was when faced with the prospect of spending the day with the woman she was seriously crushing on.

'Advantage of being your own boss.' Hayley pointed to herself. 'It's how he was able to rope me in for the day again. Not that I mind, really. But are you sure?'

Kate allowed herself a moment to fantasize Hayley looked hopeful that she might say yes. She was sure it was for more than the company. Kate desperately wanted to believe she wouldn't be just as happy to have one of the Swedish girls helping her out. 'I'm sure.'

'In that case, I'd better go find Pablo and make sure he's got some extra brushes. He'll be grateful for the help too. The sooner he can get this place up and running properly, the better. Then he can stop calling in favours from me too.' Hayley pushed off from the sink, laying a friendly hand on Kate's bare shoulder as she walked past. It was a fleeting touch and she was sure it meant nothing, but her entire body thrilled in response. She was relieved that Hayley was already on her way out of the room and couldn't see the colour flood her cheeks at the thought of those hands on her again.

She would need to go to her room and change into something more appropriate for painting. It was too much to expect that Pablo would have overalls to protect her clothing, but she did have a pair of shorts and a vest top she kept aside for some of the dirtier excursions she went on. The little denim shorts might even look stylish with a few paint marks on.

Before she could question just what lengths she would go to in pursuit of this woman, Kate washed her breakfast bowl in the sink - noting with annoyance there were already two dirty plates in there that someone had dumped. Part of her was looking forward to the next stage of her travel plan for the year, when she would have a small studio apartment to herself. The other part, the one that kept short-circuiting her brain, told her that two dirty plates were a small price to pay for a day spent with Hayley.

Back in her room, she tried on her clothes. The shorts seemed somehow shorter than she remembered, the bits of frayed denim at the top of her thighs concealing very little. She was sure that Hayley would appreciate the view, but was she being a bit too obvious? She checked the rest of her clothing choices. Over the years she had refined the art of travelling light. Packing for necessity didn't usually mean including a spare set of items suitable for random

DIY tasks that might be encountered along the way. Her original selection would have to stay, for lack of alternative, if nothing else. She tied her hair back and inspected the look one final time.

As she walked into the bathroom, ignoring the 'out of order' sign placed on the door, she felt a tug of satisfaction as Hayley looked up from her conversation with Pablo and did a double take. Some emotion darted across her face, too quick for Kate to capture, before it was shut down. One thing was certain; it was not a look of revulsion. Hayley was damn uptight, Kate could see that. Yet their first night together had shown a completely different side. The desire was there; she just had to bring it out again.

'One inexperienced painter, reporting for duty.'

'You really don't have to do this,' Hayley said again, but she was already extending a paintbrush in her direction. Eyes darted down once again to her thighs. Kate took it before anyone could change their mind.

'I keep telling you, it's no problem. Tomorrow I'll be able to get in here without feeling like I'm walking into a prison shower.'

'It's not that bad,' Hayley laughed, looking around her. 'On second thoughts, I see what you mean.' The first few layers of coat had been heavily applied to conceal the atrocity of colour chosen by the former owners of the house. They had given the walls a dirty grey look. With only a small window, it did nothing to reflect the natural sunlight coming through.

'Exactly. So what colour have you chosen Pablo?'

'Pink. For the ladies.'

'Are you serious?' Kate tried and failed to hide her

disgust. Hayley laughed.

'Of course not. *Blanco*. White for the bathroom, of course.'

'Of course.' Kate swatted his shoulder with the paintbrush. She had grown to like Pablo, even if she didn't think he was capable of running this place. Hostels took a lot of work. She'd stayed in some of the best of them and some of the worst of them over the years. It took more than a big personality on the door to keep people coming.

She couldn't tell him that though. It wasn't her place to judge and he was clearly trying hard. Hayley seemed pretty emotionally invested in the place too. Kate hoped he hadn't persuaded her to become financially invested at some point as well. The demand for the hostel was going to surge over the next year, she was sure of that, but with more people came more criticism.

And more competition.

She would try to ask Hayley about it when she got the chance.

'I leave you two ladies to work,' Pablo grinned, picking up a spare paintbrush off the floor. 'I go to the men's.' Kate assumed he meant to also paint, but wisely chose not to ask any further questions. She was just keen for him to leave so that she could get on with what she really wanted to do.

Which wasn't paint either, come to think of it.

'So how are we going to do this?' she asked, moving closer to Hayley and the tubs of paint on the floor. 'A wall each? Start off on opposite sides of the same one and move towards each other?'

'I'll take this one,' Hayley pointed at the wall with the

sink and the toilet. 'Might as well get the difficult one done first so we can take it easy this afternoon.'

'Sure. Which one do you want me to take?'

'Well, there's only one tin of paint, so you might as well take that one. Fewer trips backwards and forwards to fill the tray?'

'It sounds like you've done this before.'

'I have.' Hayley grabbed a screwdriver from the back pocket of her cargo shorts and began levering the lid off the can. 'When I bought the bar, it was at rock bottom price. The owner hadn't done anything in years. I was looking for a project.' She paused and Kate wondered what she wasn't saying.

'And you had to paint?' Kate prompted, wanting to hear more about Hayley and how she had got to be in this town.

'Oh yes. Everywhere needed painting. Of course, I started with the bar and the kitchen downstairs. All the rooms I needed to get the place open and running again. Customers through the door had to come first. Then over the next few months I got the living area upstairs habitable again. For the first eight months, I lived in the bedroom and used the bar kitchen to cook. The bathroom made this shower look like a suite at the Ritz.'

'Wow.' It must have been bad Kate thought, looking at the soon-to-be-white walls.

'It was hard work, especially as I was running the bar on my own back then. I quickly realised I needed help. I had a guy work with me for a while. He was a student studying Spanish back over in England and thought it would be a great way to spend the summer. He thought he'd spend it picking up chicks and of course, his parents were completely on board and willing to subsidise him because he'd convinced them it would be fantastic for his degree.'

'Did it work out?'

'It did for me. I had three months when the pressure was off. I could get the apartment up straight and I could learn the ropes a bit better. I'd been doing okay, but only if no-one really came in and put me under any pressure.'

'And him?'

'Have you seen the place? I still have no idea why you're here. The closest he got to chatting up a girl was someone who had come to visit her elderly mother who had retired to the sunshine. He was an optimist though. Plus I always gave him two days off in a row so he could go to one of the towns further up the coast and party the night away. I'm sure he got in his fair share of romance in the end. Just not from my bar.' Hayley tipped the paint over, filling the tray. For a second she was lost in concentration and Kate just watched her, thoughts jostling for position in her head. The more she knew about Hayley, the more she was fascinated by her.

'You must've been really brave to just do all that on your own. How old were you?' it was an innocent question, but Kate saw Hayley's shoulders tense for a second.

'I was twenty-four.'

'Wow. That's the same age I am now. I couldn't imagine doing anything like that.'

'And I couldn't imagine travelling the world.' Hayley stood and handed her the tray of paint. 'But like I said before, we're different people.'

'I can think of one thing we have in common,' Kate couldn't resist a playful smile. For a few seconds there was no response and she panicked that she'd misjudged it. Then Hayley smiled, albeit reluctantly, in response.

'We shouldn't talk about that.'

'Why?'

'You know why. Besides, you never know who might be outside listening. I don't want Pablo to overhear.'

'You weren't worried about him overhearing that night.'

'Stop it! Now start painting or we'll never be finished. Pablo will keep pestering me for help until the whole hostel is complete and as much as I would like to, I can't keep having days off just to save his arse.'

'Yes boss.'

Kate took her paintbrush and dipped it into the tray. It really had been years since she'd done anything like this. Some of her old friends from school had moved into their own houses or apartments by now. Settled down and opened tins of paint. A few of them even had kids already. Most of them were working the nine-to-five and laying down roots. Whenever she talked to them, even via email, she could sense a mixture of envy and pity at the life she was living.

At some point, they all expected her to grow up and come home. Even her parents were starting to wonder. They had stopped worrying she was doing all kinds of things for money and they knew she was sensible, but somehow it didn't seem like a real life to them. She had stopped trying to explain it to them. One day, she knew, she would have to go home and see them.

When that happened, they would expect her to stay. Then she would have to break their hearts again by leaving. It was all too painful. Now she was half a world away and home seemed ever more distant.

They painted in a comfortable silence for a little while. Kate was surprised to find it therapeutic. Even though she was always outdoors, she did very little practical work with her hands these days. She was always partially hidden behind a camera lens or a computer screen. This, she decided, felt like real work.

Damn, she sounded like her father.

'So do you have to go to the bar tonight? To work?' Kate asked when the silence became too much and her own thoughts became ominous.

'I don't have to. If we're done here early then I might. I had no idea how long this was going to take, so I thought taking the whole day was best. You've seen Pablo. Bathrooms could turn into something else at the drop of a hat.'

'He does seem to have difficulties with attention.'

'It's just his way. The Spanish building process isn't the most efficient in the world. He's brought a lot of his bad habits with him.'

'Is that what he is? By profession?'

'A builder? Yes, amongst other things.'

'I'm almost too scared to ask.'

'Oh he's a Jack of all trades, master of some.' Hayley chuckled. She stepped back to admire her handiwork around the sink and Kate realised that they were almost touching. Her breath hitched automatically. An inch more and their skin would connect.

Hayley, however, seemed unaware, engrossed in her story and the quality of her brushwork. 'He's a good guy to know. If he can't do it - at least to an approximately good job - then he'll know someone who can. In the years I've been over here, I've watched him try his hand at everything to earn some cash.'

'Is that why he's brought this place? As an investment?'

'Partially, yes. Things have been tough on this part of the coast. The economy hasn't been the greatest. The big hotels have taken a lot of the money that used to flow to the locals. Pablo is lucky, he speaks good English and a smattering of German too. But some of his brothers? I think they struggle. He tries to help them out where he can.'

'He sounds like a good guy.'

'He is. His parents are too old to work now, so I suspect he's doing his bit to help them survive as well. He doesn't talk about it much, but you live here long enough, you start to know these things.'

'What about you?'

'What about me?'

'Do you intend to stay here forever? If the economy is that bad?'

'I'm happy here. I can survive financially. What else do I need?' Hayley shrugged. It sounded overly simplistic, but Kate could almost understand. She was living the reverse lifestyle but the underlying principle was the same. She did what she loved and she made it work for her.

It really was a shame that their basic needs were the same and yet diametrically opposite.

'Don't you find it too quiet?' Kate couldn't help but push.

'Why would I?'

'There really aren't many things to do here. I mean, I think I could be occupied for a couple of months, but then what? Surely you want to do more than just work?'

'Is that how you see me? Some kind of workaholic?'

'I've met enough bar owners along the way. They're all workaholics in some form or another.'

'I have regulars. Locals. So it might seem like work to you, but it's like a big social event for me. Day after day. I don't need activities to keep me occupied. When you're older you'll understand.'

'Ouch.' It was the first explicit confirmation of Kate's suspicions. The age difference really did bother Hayley.

'What?'

'I can't believe you just pulled the age card on me.'

'I'm sorry, but it's true. The older you get, the more you see things in a different way.'

'Some would say that I've already seen more things than you. Had more experiences.'

'That's different.'

'How?' Kate turned to her. They had both stopped painting. There was a hint of challenge in her voice and she knew it.

'When you're twenty, twenty-five, you think you know who you are. But you don't. It takes time to figure this stuff out.'

'God, I don't think I've heard anything so condescending in ages.'

'I'm not trying to be. I'm just pointing out the facts.'

'You don't know me.'

'And you don't know me.' Hayley sighed and took a step back. The sink stopped her and Kate realised how close they had become during their disagreement. It had threatened to spill over into an argument and Kate couldn't understand why. Hayley clearly didn't want it to escalate any further. 'I'm sorry. Look, I'll keep my opinions to myself.'

'I don't want you to keep your opinions to yourself. I want to hear them. You're right, I don't know you, but that doesn't mean I don't want to know you.'

'But-'

'But that means I have the right to disagree as well. Two people can disagree with each other and still be friends, right?' Kate knew she should step back to give the other woman space but she stood her ground. Underneath the paint fumes, she could smell the sweetness of Hayley's skin and faded perfume.

'Of course.' Hayley smiled but there was something about her that looked... defeated. That was the best Kate could come up with. Damn this woman was infuriating. She'd never met anyone so hard to read.

'Good. Then let's carry on painting and I promise you I'll show you that just because you think I'm young and inexperienced, I know more about myself than you think. Deal?'

'Okay.'

'Good, it's a date.'

'Wait? What?' Hayley looked panicked again.

'Don't worry, no strings attached. We can just talk. I've got something to prove now.'

'After what happened between us before, do you think that's a good idea?'

'I can trust myself. Can you?' it was meant to be a joke, but it somehow fell flat. Hayley hesitated too long. No response came. For some reason, that didn't feel like a good thing. Kate knew she had to diffuse the situation. 'Look, I've got a special pass to Parque Natural Granadilla. Come with me.'

'I didn't think it was open yet?'

'It's not. They're planning to open to the public in a few months.'

'So why can you get in?'

'It will make sense when we're there. But it's legit. Totally above board.'

'If you say so.'

'It is. So how about we make a deal? I'll take you in with me and you can get a sneak preview of what it's going to be like.'

'And what do I have to do?'

'As the owner of the best bar in town, I'll leave you in charge of bringing the food and drink. We can have a picnic. I'll show you more about myself. Then you'll see I'm not really the immature backpacker you don't seem to be able to get out of your head that you think I am.'

'I never said that.' Hayley at least had the good grace to look embarrassed.

'Yeah, you did. Not using those exact words, but close enough.'

'I'm sorry. I didn't mean to offend you and I clearly have.'

'You haven't offended me. You've given me a chance

to prove to you that there's more to me than meets the eye. What more can I ask for than that?'

I guess.' The reluctance was still there, but the agreement was good enough for now.

'Good. Your tapas were delicious.' With that, Kate turned back to the painting. It felt like a victory of sorts.

She heard the soft sounds of brush on wall behind her a few moments later and allowed herself to breathe a sigh of relief. She'd been given one shot to prove herself. To show Hayley who she really was and that she was worth taking a chance on.

What happened in a month when it was time to leave again, a little voice asked her? Why was she going to all this trouble to convince Hayley when all she was going to do was walk away and leave them both broken hearted? She pushed the voice away. Emotions weren't rational. They weren't meant to be. All she knew was that she ached to feel Hayley's skin against her own one more time.

Everything else faded into nothing in comparison to that need.

CHAPTER SEVEN

Hayley checked her watch for the umpteenth time. Kate had suggested they meet at the hostel early afternoon and Hayley could drive them to the entrance of the park. Hayley had been surprised at the suggestion. She'd assumed that with the daily temperatures getting hotter as they progressed towards summer, Kate would want to set out first thing in the morning to make the most of the cool part of the day.

She reflexively checked her watch again, despite logically knowing only thirty seconds had passed since the last time she'd looked. It was a disquieting feeling, this waiting for something you had no control over. From the moment she'd agreed to go, part of her had been kicking herself for saying yes.

It wasn't that she didn't enjoy Kate's company. Over the years of so many different people walking into the bar, all colours, all nations, all ages and shapes and sizes, she'd somehow never met anyone quite like Kate before. It excited her and worried her in equal measure.

Kate clearly had something to prove. She was fun, but wasn't that how most things started out? Fun could cross the line to dangerous very quickly.

This wasn't a date, she reminded herself. It was just two people getting to know one another. Perhaps to become friends. Like she was with Pablo.

No, whatever was going on between her and Kate, it was nothing like what she felt with Pablo.

Sod it, she thought, as the urge to check her watch again made her arm wave as though she had some strange neurological twitch. She would head up to Pablo's. It didn't matter if she was early. She could always talk to him if Kate wasn't ready to leave.

Anything had to be better than driving herself mad with anticipation and fear.

#

Despite having a car, it wasn't very often that Hayley drove anywhere other than directly to the nearest city. Even then, she only did it for business when she absolutely had to. Everything she needed she could get in her small town and despite the years of living here, she never quite felt safe on the winding roads. Muscle memory from learning to drive in England made each journey one of self-doubt.

The story of her life at the moment.

Kate had been quiet on the drive, letting her concentrate. She spoke mainly to give directions from the map she was following on her phone. Although Hayley knew of the park and its recent upgraded natural heritage status, she didn't know where it was other than vaguely north of the town. She was grateful for the help and had been overcome with relief when they had pulled into the dusty makeshift car park.

'Are you sure it's okay to be here?' Hayley peered out of the window. 'No entry' warning signs were posted all over the fences. A digger was parked just inside the perimeter, but there were no other signs of life.

'Relax. I wouldn't bring you here if it wasn't. We're just early, that's all.'

'I still don't understand how you're expecting to get in.'

'I told you, I have a special pass. Oh look, that'll be him.'

'Who?'

'The guy who'll let us through the gate.' Kate opened the door and climbed out to greet the dusty red truck that had pulled up from the other end of the gravel lot. 'You grab the food. I'll go and talk to him.'

With that, the door slammed and she was gone.

Dammit. There was no turning back now. She still wasn't entirely convinced that this was all above board. She climbed out the car and was instantly hit by the dry mid afternoon heat. It felt different to the warmth of the coast. There, she was used to the cool breeze rising from the ocean, even on the hottest of days. There was wind here too, but it felt more like being blasted by a giant hair dryer. She double-checked the bag for water. She had two bottles. Kate's backpack also had more in each of the side pockets. That was good. Although the trip seemed ill-advised, Kate was at least prepared with the basics required for survival.

Her stomach clenched. She was heading into the middle of nowhere with a young girl she barely knew. Everything she knew told her that it was the wrong thing. This would have gotten her into so much trouble before. So why was she doing it?

A moment of panic and she nearly climbed straight back into the driver's seat. She could say she felt unwell. Say there was something important she'd forgotten. They'd have to return. Kate could even get a ride back with the stranger in the truck if she wanted.

It was with that thought she realised she'd tipped over into irrational again. How could she allow her to do that? Wish it on her even. Had she lost her mind entirely?

Hayley took a deep breath and grabbed the bag. She reached over and pulled Kate's backpack towards her, surprised by how heavy it was. What could she possibly need that weighed so much?

She hoped it was more water. Possibly also sunscreen. It had to be a good ten degrees warmer inland than she was used to.

As she pulled the bag free, Kate reappeared at her side. 'Let me take that.'

'Thanks. What do you have in there anyway?'

'Just my gear. Come on, he's going to show us the way in. Then we're on our own for a few hours.'

'Getting in is one thing. How are we going to get back out?'

'He's supposed to come back for us, but I told him not to worry about it. I don't think the prospect of heading back out here appealed to him much. No one is trying to get in here yet anyway. If someone really wanted to, they could climb the fence over on the other side of the car park.' She pointed to where the fence stood just behind a three-foot high rock. 'It's more of a deterrent than anything else. He's going to leave the padlock on but unlocked. We can just lock up ourselves when we're done.'

'That doesn't sound very official.'

'Who cares? If he doesn't want to do his job properly, then that's not my problem.'

'Aren't you forgetting something?'

'I don't think so?' Kate turned back to her, confused.

'What if someone else comes along, spots that the padlock isn't closed and decides to shut it?' Hayley felt proud of herself for pointing out an obvious danger.

'Then we just climb the fence. Come on, where's your sense of adventure?'

'I haven't climbed a fence since I was a kid.' Back then, it was to get out of tight spots too, but she didn't feel the need to tell Kate that.

'I know you keep banging on about how old you are grandma, but I think you should be able to manage it. *Gracias*,' she said to the man who was holding the gate for them. He was wearing a cap emblazoned with the name of the construction company, but that was about the only connection Hayley could see to the parque.

'And you're sure...' she trailed off. She sounded like a prude. And a coward. Trust didn't come easily to her. Kate had told her everything was official. It was also too late to change her mind. Kate was already through to the other side. She had no choice but to follow.

They walked in silence for a few minutes. Hayley

glanced behind her when she heard the low rumble of the truck starting up again. The noise died down as it drove away, leaving them with nothing but the almost-silence of nature surrounding them. Kate walked ahead saying nothing. The path they followed was barely that. More a foot-wide gravel path that lead from where the main entrance would eventually be to the centre of the park.

Kate turned around to her and grinned.

It took Hayley's breath away. It was as if her whole face had come to life. It made her look younger and somehow, almost impossibly, more innocent. It was such a look of unbridled joy that Hayley wasn't sure she had ever seen anything like it before. 'Isn't it amazing?'

'Um, yes?' Hayley knew it was the right answer, but she obviously wasn't seeing things in quite the same way as Kate. Instead, she was just seeing Kate.

Her brain overlaid a memory. A different face. A different time. A face she had never seen in real life, but had *been* part of her life regardless.

A face she had never seen alive.

Hayley felt her stomach roll and she clenched her fists at her side. The pain of her nails digging into her palms was enough to bring her from the memory and crash back into the real world. Kate was still smiling at her with the youthful innocence that caused Hayley so much pain.

'Come on. I've been researching it. About five minutes this way and you'll really begin to see what I mean.'

'If you say so.'

'I do say so.' With that, Kate turned back around and began to walk forwards, with a definite sense of purpose.

True to her word, as they rounded a rocky outcrop, the

scenery changed. It was no longer the dry scrub landscape Hayley saw on her rare drives to the city. Before them stood a hollowed crater. On the shaded side, protected from the full beating of the sun, the earth was covered with plants, all jostling for space. A kaleidoscope of greens and reds, flourishing in the protected earth.

She watched in silence as Kate took off her backpack and began to dig around inside. To Hayley's surprise, she pulled out a camera. An actual, honest to goodness camera with an extendable lens she screwed into place. Didn't people just use their phones these days? 'That's intense,' she said as Kate supported it with both hands.

'This?' Kate held up the camera questioningly.

'Yes.'

'Oh this is nothing. You should see what some of the other professionals have. But it's good enough for me.'

'Other professionals? Is that what you are? A photographer?'

'Not exactly. I enjoy taking photographs and I'm reasonably good at it, but I'm not like an actual professional.' She shrugged self-deprecatingly and fired off a few more shots. 'I've got a few programs on my laptop to do editing and effects, but the serious photographers have full editing suites and power computers to deal with it. I wouldn't even know where to start with those. I can just do the basics.'

'You're not a photographer. And you've made it very clear that you're not just a backpacker. So what are you?'

'That's why we're here. I want to show you. Come on.' Another flurry of shutter clicks and Kate began walking again. 'This is my favourite thing in the whole world. I get to make money by telling people about it.'

'I make money by giving people beer and food.'

'Equally noble. People will always want beer and food.'

'You sell them pictures instead? But not professional ones?' Hayley was struggling to wrap her head around the idea that this might be an actual job.

'Growing up, I always loved being outdoors. I know when people hear the Aussie accent and I say that, they assume I grew up in the outback. I was born and raised in Brissie. Brisbane. A typical city girl.'

'But you loved the outdoors?'

'I did. We'd always take trips up to Cairns. My dad loves the town for some reason, even if the people up there are madder than cut snakes. It was up there that I first went out into the rainforest. It was amazing. I can remember it so clearly. I was about ten at the time. Not much older than that for sure.' Kate paused, her eyes fixed off into the distance as she recalled the memory. 'There were signs up everywhere for the tourists. I know it sounds strange, but it was the first time I realised we had so many unique plants and animals. It's what tourists from all over the world come for, to take a gander at the roos and the koalas, but when you've grown up with them, you don't really think about it.'

'But you started to be interested in it?'

'All of it. You know what it's like when you're a kid. Something grabs your imagination and you just can't let it go. So I did my ecology and environmental conservation degree at Queensland Uni. It seemed like the right thing to do.'

'The right thing? Or the thing you wanted to do?'

'Both. Which is lucky really. Then I graduated and didn't know what I wanted to do next. I could get a job and settle down. Or I could study some more. Get a PhD, you know? Find somewhere in the world I was passionate about and study the hell out of it.' Kate paused in her story to take a few more pictures. Hayley wasn't really sure what was so fascinating about the stubbly plant, but she thought it was wise to keep her mouth shut.

'So that's what you decided to do?'

'Nope.' Kate grinned again, more devilishly this time.

'That doesn't sound good. You did all that studying and then changed your mind?' Hayley had never made it to university. It had been the goal once, but then...life had happened and changed everything.

'I decided to buy myself some time to work out which option was best. I decided to take a gap year. Go travelling. I was sure there was a big world out there that I needed to see before I could make up my mind.'

'And here you are.'

'Yep. I left Brisbane for a year. I've never been back.'

'Not even to see your family?'

'No.' For the first time, Kate sounded curt about the topic. Hayley was tempted to push, but out here in the middle of nowhere wasn't a good place to have an argument.

'So you'll just travel forever instead?' It didn't sound like a viable option to Hayley. She knew how hard it was to make money appear. She wasn't driven by it, but she knew there wasn't a magic pot of it for most people. The bar had seen its share of tough times and that was with actual people buying actual things.

'If that's what makes me happy, then that's what I'll do. I started a little blog when I first left Australia. Mostly it was to let my friends and family know what I was up to. Gloat a little. I've always wanted to be one of those people who kept a journal, but I just never had the discipline. So it was good for that too.'

'Then what happened?'

'Most of the other blogs out there focus on the fun stuff. Nothing too serious. The best traveller party spots et cetera. How to survive your first full moon party. I didn't care about that kind of stuff. I wanted to write about all these amazing places off the beaten track. Especially the ones in danger of disappearing. Either the plants or the animals being wiped out for agriculture, or logging or just for city building. Once you start looking, it's scary how quickly we're destroying the planet. It was one thing to study it, but another to see it in person. So I started writing about it.'

'Let me guess. People started reading it?' Things were starting to make a bit more sense.

'You got it. It became quite popular. I was featured a couple of times on some global cultural websites. That really sent traffic through the roof. Now I get paid to write about new places all the time. More and more people want to have experiences that don't damage the environment. They want to see animals but want to know about any hidden cruelty.'

'Ethical tourism? There are parts of the coast not far from us that are protected reserves.'

'Exactly that. So when I left, I didn't know whether to get a job or study more. I chose a third option. The education part is now one hundred per cent self-taught, but it's the perfect combination of the two.'

'So that's how you heard about the park.'

'Part of what I need to do is stay ahead of the trends. Bring new places and experiences to people before anyone else does. When I heard about the status change of the Parque, I knew I had to come and see it for myself. I contacted the guys in charge and set it all up. They want people through the gates when it opens. The preservation costs are huge. They need to be offset by tourism somehow.'

'You know a lot about this stuff.'

'I love it. That always helps with any job. You must feel the same way about the bar?'

'I did.' Hayley paused. It had been so long since she thought about it. Like a comfy pair of shoes, she'd grown into it. Life just happened and you didn't notice. Especially when things were going well. People like her, they didn't look too hard when that happened. They didn't want to jinx it. She certainly didn't.

Nevertheless, it was a fair question. As they paused for another gulp of water, she realised Kate was still waiting for an answer. 'I do love it. I just haven't thought about it in those terms for years. It's become normal. Just my life. But it still makes me happy, getting up every day and knowing that the place is mine. That between January and March I have some regular snowbirds come down from England and Scandinavia to escape the winter and recover from Christmas. Once the sunshine becomes guaranteed, I get the same people who come back every year for their holiday whilst they count down the final years towards retirement. So I love the variety and I still have familiar faces who make it feel like home.'

'It sounds nice.'

'It is. For me, at least. It can't compete with all those spectacular places on the planet for you. There's nothing much to see here.'

'There is now.' Kate waved her arms in a wide circle. 'Do you know why the park has been given its special status?'

'Not a clue. Sorry. Does that make me a bad person? I don't really pay any attention to the news.' That was an understatement.

'Three new species of plant were found here. *Three*. That's pretty impressive, given how much the world has been explored. There's still so much to see out there and there is a chance we'll destroy it before we discover it.'

'You are passionate aren't you?' Hayley couldn't help but laugh. Kate was so earnest and intense. A little furrow had appeared between her eyebrows as she talked. It was so different from the casual demeanour that had caused Hayley to mistake her for nothing but a good-time backpacker when they first met.

'Yes.' Kate put her hands on her hips in defiance. Hayley realised she'd offended her by not taking this seriously enough.

'I'm sorry. It's just I've never seen someone care about a new cactus before.'

'*Three* new. That's triple the caring.'

'I suppose. And I am interested, I promise. Please, don't let me stop you. What else is there?'

'I can't believe that three new species isn't enough for

you.' Kate picked up her bag again and continued walking. 'In addition, there are plants living here that have never been known to co-exist before. The animal life is the same old, same old, so there's nothing to surprise you with there.'

'It would have been more exciting to find a dinosaur still living in our midst, right?'

'That would have been the event of my life. But not likely.' Kate turned around and pointed the camera. Instinctively, Hayley dived out of the way. 'Stand still. I'm not good at action shots.'

'I don't want to be in any of your photos.' Her voice was high and tight. Fear shot through her as she ducked like a wounded animal.

'Don't worry, I won't use them on the site without your permission.'

'Damn right you won't.' Hayley bristled, one eye firmly on the camera direction. She wasn't going to be caught out by that cute smile.

'What's the matter?'

'Nothing. I know you're part of the selfie generation but I'm not, okay? I don't like photos.'

'Not even for-'

'No.' It came out too quickly; too harshly. Kate took a step back. There was hurt and genuine confusion in her eyes. Hayley knew she wouldn't be able to explain.

Some things couldn't be explained away with only half the story.

'I didn't mean to-' Kate tried to restart the conversation, but Hayley knew it was better just to end it there. Years of creating diversionary tactics wouldn't let her down now. She held her hand up.

'I'm self-conscious about it okay? Can we just leave it at that? Take the photos of your cactus and your craters, but please don't try to put me in any of them. Come on, I'm sure there is more of this park for you to show me. I promise that I'll listen better this time.'

With that, she gestured that the two of them should begin walking forward again. Kate looked, briefly, as if she was going to continue the discussion, but she acquiesced. She turned around and began along the path again, Hayley following just behind her. After a few minutes, Kate pointed at something and the silence that had hung between them was broken.

Hayley breathed a sigh of relief. She didn't care what Kate was saying, despite her promises to pay more attention. Instead, she was listening to the thud of her heartbeat in her ears as it steadied and dropped to a slow, dull thud rather than the staccato rhythm of fear.

#

'Don't we need to think about heading back?' Hayley asked. She'd finally been won over to the park and its secret spaces. She suspected that the sheer enthusiasm of Kate's delivery during the show and tell was a large part of that. She'd allowed herself to become distracted. She checked her watch and realised that sunset wouldn't be far away.

'We haven't eaten yet.'

'I assumed we'd grab a bite to eat in the car before we headed back.'

'No way,' Kate turned around and laughed. 'We're going to eat in about five minutes. We just need to get to the perfect spot first.'

'But it will be dark soon.'

'That's kind of the point.'

'What?'

'You really have to trust me. We're heading to there.' Kate pointed at the rocky outcrop above them. They had been moving in a steady incline but only now, when she looked behind her, did Hayley realise how high they'd climbed. 'We've been circling back round. The entrance is only a forty-five minute walk from here when we go down the other side.'

Hayley dutifully followed. The last bit was steep and she could feel the burn in her thighs. She was fit and the bar kept her strong, but it had been a long time since she had done anything even remotely resembling a hike.

Kate reached down and offered her hand. Without thinking, Hayley reached up and took it. The soft sensation of flesh on flesh reminded her of how much she wanted Kate. How much she couldn't have her. Then a gentle tug from the helping hand and she was up. As she surveyed the horizon, all thoughts of Kate temporarily left her mind. 'Wow.'

'Exactly what I was thinking.' Kate snapped more pictures, the clicker of the shutter filling the air with rapid-fire noise. 'It's as perfect as I imagined it would be. Can you believe we have this entire place to ourselves?'

'No. It's amazing. Thank you for bringing me with you.' It was like being on top of the world.

'Thank you for coming. I wasn't sure if you would. But I knew this would be an amazing chance to see it before everyone else fills the place up. It will be different once it's open to the public. For now, it feels like it's meant to feel.'

'I would never have come if it wasn't for you. Not even when it opened to everyone. I don't really do the tourist stuff.'

'I guess when it's your home, then the touristy stuff doesn't have the same appeal. Even if it meant you would see some amazing things. Come on, let's sit and eat. I've made you walk enough and listen to me ramble about plants all day. Now we can eat and watch the sun set.'

Between them, they laid out the blanket on the ground. Hayley pulled the food she had prepared from the bag. She'd watched Kate when she'd been at the bar the other day. She'd eaten the full selection of tapas, but she'd clearly liked some more than others. That much had been obvious from the look on her face. Hayley didn't know why it felt important to she make sure they were included in the selection, but she had. Kate's face lit up as she pulled out the tubs of food and poured them both a drink.

They sat in silence for the first few mouthfuls. Kate stared contentedly at the horizon and Hayley realised the walking had left her ravenous. During her pacing earlier that morning, she'd been convinced that she'd over prepared. That she'd packed far too much and it would look like she was trying too hard. Now she was convinced she could eat the entire picnic herself without any additional help from Kate.

The sun hung low in the sky, changing it from the deep blue of the day to softer pastel shades of lilac and dusty pink. The few wisps of cloud caught the light, like cotton candy brush strokes on a canvas. Hayley tried to remember when she had stopped looking at sunsets. The bar was usually busy by then. She would be frantically making sure that they were ready for the evening. She never took a moment just to look outside anymore.

That needed to change. Kate was right. The world was a beautiful place. It had been her habit to not notice the good, her one eye always on the lookout for something else.

'God these *Empanadillas* are amazing.' Kate dipped one into a sticky homemade salsa Hayley had included with their food. She popped another morsel into her mouth and chewed happily. 'I could eat them all night.'

'I'm sure you'd get bored after awhile.'

'Well I'd love to test that theory. This view and unlimited *Empanadillas* and hams. I think I'd be up for that challenge.'

'Sadly it's a long way from my kitchen to here if you turned out to be right.'

'You wouldn't make the special trip, just for me?' Kate leaned back on her elbows and grinned. The soft light of the sunset made shadows play across her face. She really was beautiful. Hayley wished she could say she wasn't, but there was no denying it. She wanted to reach out and touch her. Thoughts of their kisses replayed in her mind. It was so unfair that her heart refused to play along with what her brain knew she must do.

'Not even for you.' Hayley laughed.

'For anyone else?' It was a deliberate question and Kate stared out over the horizon when she asked it. Hayley noticed the change in her breathing, the slight catch in the rise and fall of her chest as the words came out of her mouth. Hayley knew holding back was just as much of a struggle for her too.

'No. No one else.' Hayley didn't want to lead Kate on, but she wouldn't lie to her either. She saw the smile appear on Kate's lips as she admitted there was no one else.

'Not even Pablo?' she teased with a grin.

'Definitely not Pablo. He would eat it all in the car before we even got here. Besides, he's a man, remember. Not exactly my kind of thing.'

'I didn't know if that was a definite.'

'Really?' Hayley was surprised. 'Perhaps I was doing it wrong if you hadn't worked that one out.' The words were out of her mouth before she could think about them. A blush stole to the tops of her cheeks.

'Oh, you were doing everything right.' Kate let out a throaty chuckle. 'Very right. But I don't take anything for granted. People are all different.'

'Well I can assure you there's nothing too unusual about me. I've always been into girls. Women. Other than a few forced experiments when I was a teenager, I've never doubted that I was a lesbian.'

'And everyone here knows?'

'Probably not. Without anyone in my life, it's kind of a moot point regardless. Pablo knows. I had to tell him because he kept trying to set me up with one of his brothers.'

'What did he say?'

'He was bummed because one of his sisters had just got married to a guy he didn't like. He said I should've told him sooner so he could have tried to persuade her to date me instead.'

'Oh my god,' laughed Kate, reaching out and taking the

last piece of chorizo. 'That guy is crazy.'

'He is. But he's fun to have around.' Hayley looked out and saw the sun was about to dip beneath the horizon. 'What about you?'

'What about me?'

'Are you gay? Bi? Something else?' it was the something else that worried Hayley. Not that it mattered, she reminded herself. They weren't setting out the rules of dating here.

'Oh, I don't do labels,' Kate shrugged.

'What does that mean exactly?' Hayley paused. She thought she'd given the full list of options to choose from.

'Exactly that. It doesn't feel right to me to make it a thing.'

'But isn't it 'a thing'?' Hayley felt the confusion turn to suspicion.

'Not really,' Kate shrugged. 'Calling myself something, giving myself a label won't change my emotions. It won't change the way I feel about someone. People always try to put you in a box. The biggest part of my travels have been realising that you don't have to be. So now, I don't do boxes. I don't do labels.'

It sounded, Hayley conceded, almost plausible when she put it like that. But Hayley had been around the block a time or two and had seen things for herself. As far as she was concerned, if Kate didn't want to label herself, then she was either still full of youthful defiance or there was a chance this was a new thing for her. Or, perhaps, it meant she was just open to anything, despite her assurances that the night with Hayley had been something special.

Hayley hated the thought she might be nothing more

than an experiment. A fling in a far away country that was nothing more than a story to titillate a future husband with.

No, that was unfair. She didn't know that. Still, it made her uneasy. She decided to change the topic. 'So will you come back here again?'

'The parque? Probably not, unless there's a problem with the photos when I write my article. Why, would you come back with me if I did?'

'Wouldn't you want to bring anyone else?' It was her turn for a leading question and Hayley hated herself for asking it, but she needed to know. In the same way Kate had needed to know about her. She wanted, desperately, for the answer to be no.

'No Hayley, there is no one else I'd rather be here with.'

Kate reached out and took her hand. For a second Hayley's body froze, torn between keeping it there and pulling away. Then Kate went back to looking at the final glow of the sun as it dipped beneath the edge of the world and Hayley allowed herself to breathe again. Kate's hand felt familiar in hers.

Hayley fought the memory as it returned. Even though she was awake, the thought was as persistent as when she drifted off to sleep. The knowledge that the soft fingers beneath hers had touched her skin. Had explored every inch of her body. Had been slick with desire as they'd moved between her thighs and deep inside her.

Hayley cleared her throat at the thought, her body a betrayal. The heat had built low in her belly, despite her promises that she wouldn't allow herself to feel it again.

She looked at the silhouette of Kate's body from the corner of her eye. Her breathing was deep and overly controlled; was she feeling the same memory? The last of the light bounced off perfect tanned shoulders, the shadows dipping inside the hollows of her collarbone where Hayley's tongue had once performed a dance all of its own.

Hayley forced her eyes away and back to the horizon, but not before Kate's gaze caught and held her own.

As the day turned to dusk around them, she felt as though she was trapped between two worlds. In more ways than one.

CHAPTER EIGHT

Kate listened to the soft groan of the building as she lay in the darkness. She stared up at the ceiling, aware even of her own breathing.

The silence told her it was late. The early hours of morning at least. Sleep had escaped her.

It had been nearly ten when Hayley dropped her back at the hostel. She had invited her in, admittedly under the guise of seeing Pablo, but Hayley had declined. It had been a wonderful evening. Kate hadn't wanted it to end. She'd been disappointed when they'd made it back to the park entrance and the gate was still unlocked as promised. She'd been looking forward to the fun of getting Hayley to climb the fence and behave recklessly for once.

Despite her refusal to come inside, she suspected Hayley didn't want the day to end either. The two of them had sat in silence for a while, as Kate had summoned the willpower to get out of the car and walk away alone. In the darkness it was hard to see each other clearly, but the weight of words going unsaid between them meant it didn't matter.

Kate let out a groan and hit herself on the forehead with her palm. She must be crazy.

She couldn't remember feeling like this for such a long time. It was almost like being a teenager again and developing a crush. Except, somehow it was worse.

At least with a teenage crush, you knew where you stood. Usually somewhere on the line of never gonna happen. With Hayley, it felt like it was possible, like the two of them could have something real. But Hayley was determined to keep her distance. The one night they had spent together there had been no holding back, but since then there had been nothing but.

It felt like she didn't know her and yet on some level, had always known her.

She was just being stupid and dramatic now, she decided, reaching out and flicking on the light. She blinked and squinted as her eyes adjusted. If sleep was going to be elusive and if Hayley felt like a mystery, then she should do something about it to make her less of an enigma.

Kate grabbed her phone and opened up the internet browser. She typed 'Hayley Jones' into the search engine and then realised how many there must be when over twenty million hits returned. She was going to have to be savvier than that.

But no matter how many times she typed in the name with another identifying term, nothing came back.

This was unusual. She was the master of the internet. Google was her bitch. Tonight, however, it was letting her down.

She switched over to Facebook, opening it in stalker mode just in case. She didn't need to do that so much anymore. There were fewer drunken nights trying to work out what other people were doing when she wasn't with them.

Kate began to type as she thought back to those times. Hayley thought she was young and inexperienced, that much was obvious. That because she was happy and outgoing, she could never have been through anything painful. Kate knew she could argue otherwise, but then she would have to explain things. Explaining things to others meant opening up old wounds. The wounds that felt healed until the midnight hours like this one.

After all, Kate hadn't been entirely honest about her reasons for taking a gap year after university. The job decision had been a part of it, that had been the truth, but it certainly wasn't the biggest part of the urge to run. She'd secured a place to do her Masters degree and knew she could defer for a year if she had to. No, it was her relationship that had made her pack her bags and leave behind everything she had ever known.

Kazue had been a year older. A fellow student, her brain full of advanced economics. They had so little in common, but they just clicked. Kate had been convinced that it was forever. She'd even decided to come out to her parents on the strength of their relationship.

But two years in, as Kate had been studying for her final undergrad exams, the cracks were beginning to show. They were both to blame, she knew that. When she was studying, she became hyper-focused. She had always been a model student. Under the most pressure in her life, she had developed an almost fanatical routine. She saw less and less of Kazue. Even when they were in the same room, it was as if she wasn't really there.

The fights had started. Kate had told her she just needed to be patient. That the exams would be over soon and then things would be able to go back to the way they were before. Couldn't Kazue see what a stressful time this was for her? How hard would it be to cut her some slack?

Two days before her final exam, Kate had revised late into the evening. At eleven-thirty she had realised, perhaps for the first time since exams began, that she felt alone. The confidence in her ability to pull off the final exam with the results she needed had waned. Emotionally, she felt adrift and panicked. She needed reassurance. Comfort.

She had repeatedly turned name and facts over in her head as she walked to the shared house that Kazue shared with her friends, all of them other postgrad economics students. It would be late, but she didn't think she'd mind. After all, hadn't Kazue been complaining for weeks now about the lack of sex? It would be just the thing to get her mind off the exam and also make it up to Kazue for being such a pain while she'd been studying.

The front door was open, as it always was until the last of the housemates went to bed. A big old Queenslander house, it creaked as she opened the door and stepped onto the hardwood floors. She waved at one of Kazue's friends through the kitchen doorway, failing to notice the look of panic on her face as she darted up the stairs to Kazue's room.

Despite the intervening years, Kate still felt sick at reliving the memory. It was as vivid now as the night it had happened. It was her first broken heart, and boy was it broken in an epic fashion.

She'd allowed barely a second between tapping on the door and opening. They'd been together for long enough that it never crossed her mind to wait before letting herself into the room. It was still early enough that she'd expected Kazue to be awake, even if she had gone to bed for the evening.

She was definitely already in bed. On it, at least. But she wasn't alone.

Seconds had lasted forever in that moment. The look of horror on the other girl's face at being interrupted was actually worse than the one Kazue wore at being discovered cheating. The girl was vaguely familiar. Kate was sure she'd seen her at the house before. Perhaps a friend of one of the other girls who lived there. She didn't know. She didn't care.

In that moment, she knew the life she had been planning on living, on returning to once exams were over, no longer existed. Her future changed in an instant.

Kazue had pushed herself off the other girl. 'Kate, wait-'

'If you tell me this isn't what it looks like I swear to god I'll kill you.'

'I'm sorry, I should have told you.'

'Told me?' It was then the realisation that this might not be the first time hit her. That it wasn't her neglect that had driven Kazue to this one moment of weakness. The cracks she had been willing to blame on herself, on her fanatic studying, may not have been entirely because of her. 'How long?'

'It doesn't matter.'

'Not to you perhaps. I can't believe this is happening.' Kate had put her hands over her ears, as if she could drown out the sound and make reality disappear with it.

'We should talk. Let's go downstairs okay?' Kazue had taken her hands into her own and Kate realised that she looked absurd, pleading naked in front of her. She looked across to the girl in the bed, who at least had the decency to cover herself in Kazue's sheets.

Sheets they'd bought together during a trip to a local market.

Kate thought she was going to be sick.

Yet the stranger in the bed was silent. There were no bitter recriminations. No shock. No surprise that someone had walked in on them. She knew. Knew that Kazue had a girlfriend and that girlfriend had caught them together.

It was a good thing that Kazue herself stood between the two of them. Kate had wanted to walk over to her and slap her. Hit her. Let her feel the physical pain of knowing that she had destroyed someone else's life.

Now, in a hostel thousands of kilometres away, Kate recalled the feeling with a rawness that told her that if she saw the girl now, across a crowded street or room, she would still want to hurt her. Her face was burned into her brain. It had never left.

Somehow, she'd managed to ace that final exam. With her education over, she had sat, unfeeling, as she packed up her bags ready to return home. She'd originally planned to spend the time after finals with Kazue. They would live together until they both knew for certain where next would be. Up until that night, it had never even crossed

Kate's mind that they would end up in different places. She'd been willing to do anything, be anywhere, as long as they were together.

She'd been foolish. She knew that now. But love was a powerful thing. The scars on her heart told her that it *had* been love.

At home, her parents hadn't understood the tears that happened spontaneously and for no apparent reason. She wasn't foolish enough to pretend they weren't at least partly happy that the relationship was over. They'd never been openly hostile, but she knew them well enough. Being a woman was bad enough, but Kazue's pretty Asian skin was another nail in the coffin as far as they were concerned. Kate was a pretty girl. Now that the foolishness was out of her head, she could settle down and find herself a nice Outback Jack.

A college fling. That was all it was to them. It became easier just to ignore their beliefs while she concentrated on the slightly more important thing of what the hell she was going to do next. How she could begin to pick up her life.

How she was going to make it a brand new one.

That was where the no labels approach was born. It had made things easier during that time, caused less pained discussions. Then it had stuck. It was about not tying herself down. It was about allowing herself to be free again.

After four weeks at home, the crying happened less often. Kazue had been in touch twice. The first time, motivated by guilt, was to see how she was doing. Kate had wanted to know if the girl in her bed was now a permanent fixture in amongst her sheets, but she had somehow stopped herself from asking.

The second time, it was to return some things that belonged to Kate. It wasn't much, but Kazue needed to know if she wanted to collect them. Kate hadn't wanted to, but they were parts of her life. Kazue wouldn't keep them. She had gone to the house to collect them, both relieved and angry when Kazue wasn't there and one of her friends - the one who had been at the kitchen table that night - apologetically handed them over.

She put down her phone and stared at the hostel ceiling again. Hayley, it appeared, was a difficult woman to find. To all intents and purposes, she seemed to live off the grid. That was unusual. And particularly unhelpful in giving her mind something useful to focus on.

Since the night that had upended her life, Hayley was the first person she'd met who she was interested in enough to chase. Of course, it would feel foolish to admit that to her out loud. The odd kiss here and there as she moved from town to town didn't count. It had never even gone further than a kiss.

As soon as things started to pick up pace, memories of Kazue's mouth, her lips on her skin, her fingertips running over her body, always returned with painful humiliation. It was a serious mood killer. Kate could never get over it. She'd grown used to making excuses and quickly running away.

With Hayley, it had been different. The memory had appeared, as she had expected it to. But then Hayley had tugged on her bottom lip with her teeth and she'd seen something in her eyes that told her this was a new start for both of them.

There are just some moments when everything makes sense.

Feeling Hayley pull her body down onto the bed was one of them.

This bed.

Kate gritted her teeth with longing at the memory. She would do anything for Hayley to be in here now, rather than being an elusive ghost.

The frustration did nothing to quell the fire and temptation. She had switched on the light with the intent of turning Hayley into something more tangible, but somehow had been left with more questions than answers. There was nothing even to associate her with the bar. She knew it was possible to be discrete on the internet, but she just wasn't used to someone being so concerned about their privacy. She'd heard it was possible, sure. But living out of sight? That was just an alien concept to her.

Kate got out of bed and walked over to the cupboard where she kept her camera. She took it out and turned it on. The three inch LCD screen gave her a great view of the shots she had taken, without having to download them onto her laptop. She returned to bed and began clicking through the photographs from earlier that day.

True to her word, she hadn't consciously taken any pictures of Hayley after being so explicitly requested not to do so. But, as she'd hoped, there were a handful where she had inadvertently caught her at the edge of the frame. She zoomed into these on the small screen, looking at pictures of Hayley when she had been unguarded.

That was it, she realised. If there was a word she was looking for to describe the other woman whenever they were together, then it was guarded.

Kate guessed she must not be the only one with a broken heart. Perhaps there had been someone else once. A dead wife perhaps? That sounded suitably dramatic enough to turn someone into a public recluse. Hayley definitely existed on the surface of life. Her emotional depths were out of bounds to everyone.

Of course, Kate had hardly been forthcoming with her own hopes and dreams so far. She could hardly blame Hayley for not opening up on what was technically their first date.

That was how she would always see today. Their first date.

That also implied there would be a second. As she selected another image and zoomed, Kate knew that she would do just about anything in her power to ensure that it happened. The intensity of her feelings enthralled and terrified her. The wound that had been Kazue had finally begun to heal and if anyone was going to be the glue to mend her broken heart, then Hayley was that person.

Thoughts of the future crowded her head and she pushed them away. She had planned for it once and look how that had turned out. No, it was better not to think about it. There were bridges you could only cross once you came to them.

The sound of someone getting up from one of the dorm rooms and heading to the bathroom made her check her watch again. If she didn't sleep soon, then tomorrow was going to turn into a long and painful day. She switched off the camera and returned it to its spot in the cupboard. The pictures of Hayley would still be there in the morning.

As she settled down and tried once again to fall asleep, she wondered if down at the bottom of the hill, Hayley was having a frustrated, sleepless night of her own.

CHAPTER NINE

The camera flashes blinded her view. They came thick and fast as she pushed her way through the crowd. The police officers either side of her were supposed to keep the people away, but they let her be jostled enough to let her know they all suspected her as well.

Why did no one believe her?

She was a witness, nothing more. Every flash made her feel like she was the one on trial. She would be sitting in the witness box, not the dock. The man in front stopped asking her questions.

He began to accuse her.

The verdict came in. She was still sitting there, still saying she didn't know anything.

One by one, they yelled.

Guilty.

Guilty.

The final juror stood up and looked at her. It was Kate. Dead Kate. As she opened her mouth, Kate shifted to the girl, the final girl who had died.

Guilty.

Hayley sat up in bed, sweat running down her back. Thin pyjamas stuck to her skin. Her heart was beating so fast it felt like a tight band of steel had encircled her chest and it squeezed. Contracted. Getting air into her lungs was impossible and the panic began to claw at her throat.

Her hands gripped the sheets, cramping in fear.

It was just a bad dream, she told herself. The urge to scream for help remained overwhelming.

She needed to calm down.

She turned on the light with trembling hands and looked around the room, trying to find something to focus on. She saw a coffee cup on the nightstand and stared at it intently, slowing her breathing as her therapist had taught her to do long ago. Eventually, after what felt like forever, the walls stopped closing in. She felt calm enough to just feel sick, rather than terrified.

She had gone to sleep with the air con running, but her skin was covered with the cold sweat of fear.

Hayley ran her hands over her eyes. It had been over a year since she'd had a nightmare as intense as that. Her past continually invaded her dreams, but never enough to feel devastating.

In the beginning, those debilitating nightmares had come once a week, sometimes more. Then they faded to once a month as she began to heal, piece by piece.

Only when she came here did they go away completely for months on end. That was when she knew she'd found the place she needed to stay. She would never go back to England again.

She hadn't had a cigarette in fifteen years, but she wanted one so desperately. She always did when a nightmare like that happened. Something to make the shaking go away. In the jittery aftershocks of adrenalin, it felt good to have something to do with her hands.

She got out of bed, grabbed her robe and opened the doors to the small balcony that sat above the bar. She hardly ever went out there. She kept her life too busy with the bar to sit and relax. A small plastic chair was her only concession to its status as a usable area.

Tonight she needed to feel the fresh air. She needed to breathe the clean sea breeze and remind herself she was here and not there anymore.

The night was chilly on her damp skin and she tugged the robe tighter around her as she sat down. Lights were still on further along the coast, up on the hill where the main hotels of the resort were built. In her little part of town, it was darker. The locals slept more soundly in their beds. As she looked out over the ocean into the inky blackness, she could see the light of the moon dissecting the darkness where water and sky met. Above her a thousand stars twinkled, making her feel small in the universe.

Small and insignificant. That was exactly how she wanted to feel right now.

Her hands fiddled with the edge of her robe. It was no surprise, now she was fully awake and free of its clutches, that a nightmare had paid her a visit. She had known from the moment she'd laid eyes on Kate it would open up old wounds. She'd known and she had done it anyway. She only had herself to blame.

Of course, the courtroom of her nightmares was not identical to the one she had experienced in real life.

Back then, fifteen-year-old Hayley Jones had been Rachael Taylor Chapman and everyone knew her name. More importantly, they knew her father's name. His picture was on the front page of every newspaper, broadsheet or tabloid.

Britain's most notorious serial killer since the Yorkshire Ripper had finally been caught.

He'd denied it all, of course, in the beginning. A long-distance lorry driver, he had argued that the routes he took up and down Britain, down to mainland Europe and back, were routes taken by thousands of others. That they had the wrong man.

Hayley had wanted so desperately to believe him. He was a good father. He worked hard. He was her dad. He had been away from home a lot while she was growing up, but that was the price you had to pay to do the job. He had taken her with him sometimes, during the school holidays. They had slept in the cab, parked in truck stops overnight. It had felt like one big adventure the first time she had sat up front with him. The last time she'd travelled with him had been only a few weeks before the police had turned up at their door with a warrant for his arrest.

That was, she knew, why so many people believed she had been a part of it on some level.

Her mother, consumed by a guilt that wasn't hers to carry, had killed herself the night before the guilty verdict was delivered.

With one parent dead and the other looking down the barrel of consecutive life sentences, four months before her sixteenth birthday, Hayley had found herself entirely alone.

She finished out the school year and somehow still managed to get good grades, but foster homes didn't really matter when you were so close to being an adult. Instead, she ended up in a grimy one-bed council flat in the very worst part of town. There was no support. No counselling. Not much to do when there was no one around to help you and your friends no longer wanted to know you.

Those years haunted her the most. There was worse to come, but it wasn't like the terror of those times. When the shit really hit the fan, she was older. Tougher. But back then, she was still a raw half-girl, half-woman living in a strange place, the fear of being singled out for retribution always not far behind.

They had been the days of looking over her shoulder.

The days of only going out after dark so she wouldn't be recognised. Of chip shop food and cheap booze from the local shop that never asked for any ID.

In the end, she cut her hair and dyed it pink. She changed her style to something that the young Rachael would never have worn. She was still a long way from becoming Hayley Jones, but the first sense that she could be someone else, someone who wasn't just the daughter of a murderer had been born.

Eventually she'd got a job behind a bar. With no friends, she was willing to do all the shifts that no one else wanted. She worked hard and saved up her money. The first thing she really bought for herself was the Celtic knot tattoo Kate had traced almost reverently on their one night together. It had hurt getting it done, but it was a good kind of pain. It was the pain of a new beginning. The guy who did it wasn't the best in town. He was no artist, but that didn't matter to her. It was the design that mattered. A symbol of inner strength. The talisman that signalled she was rising from the ashes.

She started seeing a therapist to help her with the nightmares. Back then, they still happened frequently enough that she would spend some weeks going from work to sleep in a constant state of exhaustion. Finally, she began to face up to what her father had done.

He'd confessed, in the end. Her thin security blanket of denial over the matter was long gone.

And beneath it, she found a new reason to fear. Coming to terms with the fact she was gay terrified her. Not because of the usual reasons. She didn't have to deal with peer pressure or religious relatives. It was the knowledge that if she'd liked boys instead, then it would make her less like him.

But no, she liked girls. Worse, despite forcing herself to try to feel otherwise, the girls she found herself attracted to, the pretty ones with the long hair and the open smiles, were all too similar to the ones he had lured into his cab in the darkness and killed.

On the balcony, Hayley shuddered from the memory. She genuinely liked Kate, but she was too much like the ones that had gone before. The ones he had taken. Kate made the nightmares come back to life.

Of course, Hayley had never had a single impulse to do any of the things he did. Her temper, during those late teenage years, came from the hurt and isolation of being alone and vulnerable, not some darker desire. Once her life began to make sense again, that anger went away. Occasional medication kept the anxiety in check. Now, she didn't even like to argue. She didn't like the heightened rush of emotions. It was why she went along with Pablo's harebrained schemes so easily and why she had tried to placate Kate each time it seemed they were veering towards a disagreement.

She didn't want to be a murderer. She didn't want to be like him.

Even if she knew it to be true, that didn't mean everyone else did. The rumours never really went away. Perhaps, if he'd never taken her with him on his jobs, then the idea would never have crossed anyone's mind. But he had, and they'd been pleasant, uneventful journeys at the time. In the years since, she had tried to remember what it was like. If there were any warning signs. He'd not so much as picked up a hitchhiker when she was with him. Instead, it was listening to the radio and watching the trees on motorway embankments go by. In hindsight, they were dull trips. Mundane, really.

There was never any sense that behind her, in the back of the cab, when she went on that last trip with him, at least five girls had died in the very spot where she went to sleep.

Hayley retched. The feeling never got any better. It never stopped her feeling dirty.

It was that macabre fact that had kept the press hounding her for years. Whenever the anniversary of the guilty verdict came round, one newspaper or another would print an article on him and she would be implicated in some subtle way. It was all very cleverly done - at one point she had even seen a lawyer in the hopes she could sue and stop them for good - to keep the misery alive in the public's mind.

Then, she had the break she so sorely needed. One tabloid hack of a paper went too far. Her phone was tapped, the calls monitored in the hope that she would communicate with her father. It was through sheer chance that it was found out, in relation to another big news story involving a politician and his inflatable friend, but it was enough for her to get a payout.

Suddenly she had the kind of cash that working behind a bar was never going to provide, even if she worked until she was sixty and saved every penny. Enough money, she knew, to buy a new life somewhere else.

It had been surprisingly easy to stop being Rachael Taylor Chapman and become plain old Hayley Jones. All the official documentation was still in her old name, but she soon found out that when you met people for the first time, they never asked for proof. They took the name you gave them as truth, without question.

Her whole life here was built on a lie, but it was a lie that gave her a chance at living again.

Damn, she could really do with a cigarette.

This was the closest she had been in years to being discovered and it was all a mess of her own making. Pablo loved her like a brother, but he was so caught up in his own world that he didn't ever question her about hers. When he did, it was only at a superficial level. She had become adept at having conversations where she spoke and yet somehow still said nothing at all.

Kate, she knew, was different.

Kate wanted to date her, be with her, *know* her. It was more than just sex.

This was both a good and a bad thing, depending on which one of Hayley's emotions were in charge. It was great that someone like Kate, who she found curiously interesting and attractive, felt the same way about her. That she didn't just want a quick fling. She was sure that would be how other people would feel about this unexpected turn of events. The sex had been great, but would it have been better to live with a lifetime of wistful regrets than face the reality of this thing she could never have?

She looked at the incandescent fire of the Milky Way swirling its band overhead. This was a sight she had never seen growing up. If the truth got out about who she really was, then she would have to say goodbye to the world she was only just discovering. Why had she never taken the time to appreciate it more?

That was what she couldn't understand about Kate. She lived a life of adventure, if one chose to look at it that way. Hayley saw it as a life where you had to keep starting over. Her only experience of that was steeped in pain and fear.

Hayley knew she was wilfully ignoring the good points and emphasising the bad. She had made a promise to herself, once she had opened the bar and fully transitioned from Rachael to Hayley, that she would always choose herself and her freedom over anything else. That it was better to spend a lifetime of lonely nights than a lifetime of fearful ones.

Yes, Hayley had chosen not to be afraid and for years,

it had worked. Now Kate had come along and she was terrified once again.

She'd avoided the news after the first few weeks of being in town. Sometimes a customer would bring a copy of the worst kind of tabloid into the bar to read with their beer and she would force herself not to look at the headline. She needed no reminders of a life back home.

Only one person knew where she was: her lawyer. The two of them had actually formed a close friendship throughout the newspaper trial and it made her happier to know that he was bound by client confidentiality. It made it easier for her to trust him. He got in touch maybe once a year, just to check that things were okay and catch up on any minor legal matters. When he did, she guessed it had been prompted by her father making the news again and a subsequent reference to her had appeared.

It annoyed her that her father was now throwing himself into the spotlight. She had hoped, erroneously, that he would quietly live out the rest of his life in repentance and regret. Instead, prison had brought out the worst in him. Or, perhaps, he no longer had to hide the man he had been all along. There had been fights, which he usually won thanks to the years overcompensating for trucking by bodybuilding, and hunger strikes that always seemed less successful. The one thing that hadn't been a lie all along was his love of food.

Years of not being able to find her, of being unable to provide a new and harrowing picture of her trying to live a normal life, meant that the heat had died down. The more time went by, the more the media turned to him and away from her.

Hayley wasn't stupid. She'd seen the circus that happened around the tenth anniversary of his conviction. The parents of the girls he had killed had given interviews about how their lives had been destroyed forever.

Now, she knew, the twentieth anniversary was coming up. Could it really have been that long? It made her feel old, being thirty-six, when she was using the stolen lives of others as her marker for the passage of time. The frenzy would start again. Soon, they would be reviewing his sentences and deeming him still to be a danger to the public. There was no other viable option. She wanted him kept behind bars as much as anyone else.

It was a heavy burden for her to carry alone.

It was too much of a burden to share with anyone else.

Kate shouldn't have to deal with this kind of thing. Hayley didn't want to tell her the truth and watch as the horror spread over her face and she walked out the door. Because, really, wasn't that the only way this could end?

No, a stern voice reminded her, the real ending would be Kate telling everyone else. Then the bar, Pablo, and all the tentative steps towards happiness she had finally taken would be gone forever.

She'd survived so much hatred and loss when she was younger.

She wasn't sure she would survive it again.

CHAPTER TEN

Kate had a plan.

In the early hours of the morning, when she had turned off the light and yet somehow sleep remained elusive, she'd gone over and over the conversations they'd shared during their amazing day together.

That was how she saw it, anyway. Amazing. She hoped Hayley felt the same way, but she knew just the experience of the park itself was fantastic as far as she was concerned. Hayley had been the icing on the cake.

She had gone over every word they'd said, remembering each smile, each joke. Each casual brush against each other when they were walking, or when Kate reached out to show her something.

They were her favourite memories of the previous twenty-four hours. Those moments when their skin touched and the electricity that flowed between them told her that this was more than just her imagination. More than just wishful thinking.

In amongst the reminiscing, it dawned on her that she'd played her strongest card at the start.

An exclusive, private showing of the park before it opened to the public was the one unique thing she had to offer. Hayley had been so reluctant to give in to her charms that she'd decided to go big or go home. Now she had nothing else to win her over with for their second date.

That was when her thoughts had returned to the conversation and saw Hayley had revealed a little bit about herself that Kate knew she could use.

All she had to do was convince Hayley that she wanted to do it with her.

'Good morning,' she said brightly, bouncing through the doors into the bar. She saw the automatic smile that appeared on Hayley's face before it was pushed back down into something more neutral. Not an ideal response, but Kate wasn't going to let that stop her.

'Hi.' Hayley's response was measured. Kate ploughed on as if she hadn't noticed.

'Isn't it a beautiful day out there? I can see why you love this place.'

'Not today I don't. Marco forgot to tell me that we're almost out of cava, so I've spent all morning trying to sort out an emergency supply. Since the Prosecco boom people are drinking it like it's going out of fashion. Anyway, what can I do for you? Coffee? Breakfast?'

'Just a flat white please, if it's not too much trouble to ask you to go off menu for me again? I'm going to hold out on the pastries until my willpower crumbles. Am I okay to take a table and work in here today?'

'Of course. Take a seat and I'll bring it over to you.'

'Thanks.' Kate, however, did not take a seat. Instead, she stayed propped up at the bar, watching Hayley make the drink. She could watch her all day, she thought dreamily, before mentally slapping herself across the face with a warning to snap out of it. 'Did you enjoy yourself yesterday?'

'I did. Thank you.' Hayley threw a smile her way from the coffee machine. 'I would never have done it on my own. You seemed to enjoy it too.'

'I did. It was amazing.'

'And I didn't distract you from your work too much?' Hayley placed the coffee down on the counter in front of Kate. 'I mean, you didn't have to waste time explaining things to me when you could have been making notes, or whatever it is you usually do on these things?'

'Of course not. It actually helped.'

'It did?'

'Yes.' Kate took a sip of the hot coffee. She was already looking forward to the joy of real caffeine flooding her system. 'I visit these places already knowing more about them than most people. Having to explain things to you, or point things out you wouldn't have noticed, it helped me to see things through a fresh pair of eyes. It's given me a better idea of how to write the article now.'

'Can I read it? When you're done?' it was an innocent question, but Kate could sense something else brewing under the surface.

'Of course. How about I let you read the first draft if I finish it here today? It won't be exactly the same as the final one and it will need a bit of polish, but it will give you a good idea. That way, you can read it before the rest of the world.'

'That would be great,' Hayley let out a genuine smile.

'No worries,' Kate took another sip of coffee, wondering if now was the time to execute phase two of the plan. It was still quiet in the bar but if things picked up, she might not get the chance to talk to Hayley again today. She had a feeling that the first response to the question would be no. Kate had to build in some extra time to persuade Hayley to her way of thinking.

Ah, what the hell. 'In fact, I was thinking, because it was so useful, you might be able to help me out again.' Subtle. That was good.

'I doubt it. If you're expecting me to remember all those Latin names you told me yesterday then you're going to be bitterly disappointed. Biology wasn't even my favourite subject at school.'

'No, nothing that complicated. What are you doing Monday?'

'What?' Hayley seemed surprised that Kate was asking her out again.

'I need to write about something more universally appealing that people can do when they're in town. Are you free on Monday?'

'I have to work here. I've already taken too much time off to help Pablo. It's clear that Marco is getting overwhelmed with the extra shifts if he's forgetting things like cava.'

'From what I've seen of Marco, I suspect it was more to do with the pretty girl drinking the cava than it was to do with overwork.'

'You may have a point. But I'm not sure I can take the chance. Why do you want to know anyway?'

'I want to go on a dolphin watching excursion.'

'Seriously?' Hayley looked at her like she had gone mad. 'Why would you want to do that touristy piece of crap?'

'Because, technically, I am a tourist?' Kate countered. 'I'm guessing by the phrase 'piece of crap' that you've never done one?'

'No, I haven't.'

'Good. I told you I needed a fresh pair of eyes. I've done about seven now, all in different places. I need someone who is new to the whole experience.'

'Dolphin watching hardly screams eco tourism to me.'

'You're right.' Kate was prepared for Hayley's arguments. 'I've been doing my research and there is a new operator opening up over in Playa de Guayedra. That's the next beach along, right?'

'Right.'

'It's a more eco-friendly one. Family owned and operated. They don't use sonar or any of that kind of shit to track the dolphins down. There's no 'see the dolphins or get your money back' guarantee because they're doing it the old-fashioned way. I won't promote it as a better alternative unless I've tried it myself.'

'I've worked with punters for long enough to know they are always going to go for the money back guarantee option if there is one. Don't waste your time.'

'Exactly. I need to see if it has more going for it than just dolphins. It has to be a full experience. I need a second opinion. I can't do it on my own.'

'I'm sure you can,' Hayley laughed.

'Okay, I don't want to do it on my own. Come on, it will be fun. It really will help me with my research. Don't you want local, traditional family businesses to thrive?'

'Of course I do.'

'Will you at least think about it? Don't answer right away. Tell me at the end of the day, when I've written my article.'

'Fine, I'll think about it. But don't assume that means I'm going to say yes.'

'Thank you.'

'Now go grab a table before everyone comes in. That one over there has a power socket underneath if you need it.'

'That would be perfect.' Kate picked up the remains of her coffee and carried the cup over to the table Hayley had suggested. It was far enough away from the window to avoid the glare of the sunlight on her screen, but still afforded her a view of the world outside passing by. It was a happy balance and had the added bonus of providing a distraction from simply staring at Hayley.

\#

As always, once she actually began to piece the article together, she lost track of time, totally absorbed in her work. There were so many things she wanted to write about, but she could only select the most important things. It was difficult to choose and she barely noticed that the coffee cup next to her was never empty when she reached for it.

'Am I okay to interrupt?' the voice made Kate look up and it took a second for her eyes to focus on Hayley standing next to her.

'Sure. I was - shit, is that the time?'

'That's what I thought. You should take a break. You've been staring at that screen now for three hours and I'm not sure I've seen you look up once. That can't be good for your sight.'

'It really isn't.' Kate balled her hands into fists and rubbed eyes. They felt gritty and sore. 'I should take a break.'

'I'm about to have lunch. Do you want to come with me? There's a table and chairs behind the building if you want a change of scene?' It came out in a rush, as if Hayley was already changing her mind.

'Um, sure. If that's okay?'

'Of course. You can leave your laptop in the office so you don't have to worry about it.'

'Thanks.'

Kate didn't know if it had been a busy day for Hayley, she had been so wrapped up in her own world. As she looked around the room now, she could see that only a handful of tables were occupied after the main lunch service. The transition from cafe to bar would soon begin. She followed Hayley behind the counter, feeling like she was heading into some new, almost forbidden, territory. She ignored Marco's raised eyebrow and cheeky grin as she walked past.

'That door there is to the office. I mean that in the loosest possible terms. But you can dump your stuff in there.'

'Thanks.' Kate pushed open the door. The room was tiny, with a desk and chair, but not a lot else. It felt dark and claustrophobic. She'd never had to work in a cubicle, but after years of coffee shops and open plan co-working spaces, she didn't think she would ever be able to live that way of life. She hastily dumped her bag on the desk and returned to the kitchen.

On the counter were two plates. Cheese, cold cuts and crusty fresh bread sat on each. 'I went for the basics, I hope you don't mind?' Hayley asked, picking them up. 'I don't have much time for lunch, so quick and easy is always the way.'

'That's perfect.'

'Follow me, we can sit out the back and enjoy the heat. It's actually quite pretty if you ignore the empty beer barrels.'

Kate followed Hayley through the kitchen doors to a makeshift patio area at the back of the building. A small plastic table with two chairs sat in the shade, facing out over a small area filled with beer barrels and empty crates. A high fence at the back made it relatively private.

Hayley placed the plates on the table and took a seat. 'I told you it wasn't much to look at.'

'I like it. It's peaceful.' It wasn't a lie. She took a bite of the bread and looked around. Given that Hayley had owned the place for so many years, there weren't many personal touches. This was the closest space she had to a garden, but the only thing to indicate it could be used for such a purpose was a small tree in a giant pot that Kate couldn't immediately identify. Its fruits reminded her of Chinese lanterns. 'What's that?'

'It's a tangelo tree.'

'A what now?' Kate took another bite of bread and some cheese. She took a moment to savour the taste before turning her attention back to what Hayley was saying.

'A tangelo tree. It's not native to the region, but it suits the climate well. I wanted something unusual. It was a strange whim, years ago.'

'I'm not sure as an ecologist I can condone the introduction of non-native species.'

'Then it's a good thing I'm not asking for your approval,' laughed Hayley, popping a wafer-thin slice of *Jamón* into her mouth. 'Besides, the fruit is delicious. You haven't complained when you've been eating it.'

'I've eaten it?' Kate shook her head, surprised. All the food Hayley had given her had been of the strictly savoury variety.

'Yes. On our picnic, yesterday. I used them in one of the dipping sauces.'

'Wow.'

'Here, let me get one.' Hayley stood up and walked over to the tree, assessing the available fruits before selecting one and tugging it free with an expert twist. 'There,' she said handing it over. 'Try it.'

Kate handled the fruit, turning it over to feel the peel in her hands. The orange was so vibrant it almost felt unreal. But whereas an orange was a perfect round shape, the top of this fruit had something decidedly weird at the top. The only word that came to mind was 'nipple', but she decided to keep that thought to herself. Instead, she peeled the fruit to reveal the segments inside. As her nails pierced the skin, a fine spray of zest filled the air. She popped a slice into her mouth, not knowing what to expect. Her mind kept going back to the nipple and couldn't predict what her tongue would feel.

It was sweet, less like an orange and more like one of its smaller equivalents. Was it like a tangerine or a satsuma? Kate wasn't sure she would know the different between the two regardless. But it was so juicy her mouth filled with flavour. 'This is delicious.'

'I know. I don't use them in the bar food unless I get a particularly bumper crop. It doesn't happen very often, but if I've got some left over I make a marmalade towards the end of the season. At this time of year, I add them to the sauces I make for my own food. There's nothing quite like something sweet to offset salty tapas.'

'You are so right.' Kate popped another segment in her mouth. 'I still don't condone it though.'

'And I still don't care. You can hand it back if you're morally offended.'

'I wouldn't go that far. I can't believe I've never tried these.'

'I think they're Californian. I could be wrong. That sort of thing has never mattered to me as much as how it tastes.' Hayley went back to eating the last few bites of her own lunch. She'd eaten for efficiency rather than pleasure. 'Speaking of which, I should probably thinking about getting back.'

'Already?' Kate's own plate was still half full.

'Yes, already.'

'That's hardly a lunch break. You practically inhaled your food.'

'It's more than I usually get. Most of the time I just eat in the office so I can do the paperwork at the same time. This has been a nice change for me. But you're right, it wasn't long. You take as long as you need out here to give your eyes a rest. Just come back in when you've had enough of the heat.'

'Thank you.'

'No problem.' Hayley stood up and picked up her plate. Kate knew it was a good time to push a little more. They might not get any time alone again today. 'So have you thought any more about my offer?'

'What offer?'

'Don't feign ignorance. The dolphin watching excursion.'

'Were you actually being serious about that?'

'Of course I was.'

'I told you, why would I want to go on a dolphin watching trip with a bunch of tourists? Really?'

'And I've told you, it's a new company. There won't be many other tourists yet. You had a good time yesterday, didn't you?'

'Yes, but that was different.'

'No, it wasn't. I wouldn't ask you to do it if I didn't think you would have a good time. You don't get seasick do you?'

'Not that I know of.'

'Then what is there to lose?'

'A day of my life watching people get drunk at sea and then throw up over the side?'

'Don't get me wrong, I'm sure that happens on the larger boats. In fact, I've been on a few trips that were more about the free beer than the dolphins. I don't think this one will be like that or I wouldn't go. Come on, how about it?'

'Do I have a choice?' Hayley rolled her eyes, but Kate could tell she was close to caving.

'You always have a choice. I promise it will be a fantastic day. And if I turn out to be wrong, then I'll find some way to make it up to you.'

'You should be careful making promises. They could get you into all kinds of trouble.'

'It will be worth it. So?'

'Alright, alright. I'll come, but only so you'll stop asking me about it.'

'If you say so.'

'What? Are you saying you won't just keep nagging me until I give in anyway?'

'That's true, but part of you wants to come, admit it.'

'Never.' Hayley walked back to the doorway that led inside. 'And stop being so cocky. It doesn't suit you.'

With that she was gone, leaving Kate alone with the remains of her lunch and a smug look on her face.

Date number two was good to go.

CHAPTER ELEVEN

Hayley sat back in the comfortable seat, her arms stretched over the side of the boat. It had been years since she had been on the water. She preferred looking at it from the safety of dry land. It wasn't that she was scared of it, or anything like that. She was a perfectly competent swimmer. Somehow it never tugged on her heartstrings in the way it called to some people. The ocean was a thing of beauty to watch, not sit on.

Despite her reservations, she had conceded within the first hour of the trip that Kate was once again right. It was becoming a disconcerting pattern and did nothing to stop her from liking Kate even more. She had spent another guilt-ridden morning before the two of them met up, chastising herself for doing something she shouldn't do. The more she told herself it was wrong to spend time with Kate, wrong to encourage her friendship and keep the hope alive there might be something more, the more she found herself unable to keep away.

The boat was small and its owner was someone she recognised from the town. Not that he did any talking, other than a gruff *hola* before he disappeared into the cockpit to pull them out of the harbour. It was his niece, fluent enough in both English and German, who was playing the role of tour guide.

Hayley watched as Kate effortlessly extracted information from her, including the detail of the familial relationship between the two. There was something about Kate's laid back, friendly manner that made people respond in kind. She needed to remember that the next time she felt the urge to open up any more than she already had.

The tour company, if it could be called anything so grand, had been running since the end of the previous main season, but she'd never heard of them. If the captain of the boat was the man behind the venture, she suspected he had even less marketing skills than she did. He would need to get the word out more if he hoped to compete with the big boats in Playa de Guayedra.

Then again, wasn't that what people like Kate were for?

She watched behind her reflective sunglasses as Kate chatted away, using her hands for emphasis. The big camera she had used at the park had been replaced by a smaller model. One that, Hayley assumed, was water resistant. She had no idea how much cameras were worth these days, but Kate's other equipment seemed too expensive to risk ruining during an encounter with the sea.

As she stared at Kate, she felt the familiar creep of lust that happened when she looked at her for too long. It was driving her insane, but her only way of dealing with it so far had been to occupy her hands and mind with something else. Serving behind the bar, leaving the room, those were tactics she had fallen back on.

On a boat, thighs pressed next to each other as it rocked backwards and forwards, there was nowhere to run.

Hayley swallowed, trying not to stare too hard at Kate's tanned, toned legs against her own skin. They were the colour of brown sugar and just as sweet. Damn it, this was nothing short of torture.

She looked away, determined to distract herself. There were only two other couples on the boat and a family with two children under ten. The children were staring at the screens of either phones or portable game devices. The trip was wasted on them. They had no interest in the boat itself, or the view over the ocean as they clipped along. She presumed, should the dolphins actually appear, that they would look up, but she wasn't confident enough to bet on it. The parents weren't talking to each other either.

So much for family holidays together. Was that how they were these days?

For a second she remembered her own childhood at the beach with her mother and father in Devon, but she pushed the thought away before it could take hold. When she remembered her early life, even the good times, it could send her into a downward spiral that would last for hours. It wasn't fair to do that today, not when Kate had gone to so much trouble for them to have a nice day out. Ice cream cones and mini pots of shrimp were a part of her past and she needed to stay fully in the present.

It was actually nice, having a few empty seats on the

boat. It wasn't that big to begin with. Kate had managed to discover that at maximum capacity, it could take twenty people. Hayley was convinced not everyone would get a seat if that happened. As it was, she could get close to Kate, without having to get close to anyone else.

Kate finished the conversation and their erstwhile tour guide left to speak to her uncle. As she disappeared out of view, Kate turned to Hayley with a smile. 'See, this is nice, isn't it?'

'It is. I'm not sure I'd enjoy it as much in high season though.'

'Nor me. I try to do the more mainstream activities when no one else is around. You get so much more out of it that way. The tour guides can actually take the time to speak to you. It's usually cheaper too. Always need to be budget conscious when you're travelling.'

'Plus you made yourself a little friend.' Hayley nodded in the direction of the cockpit.

'Jealous?' Kate poked her in the side with her elbow.

'Not at all. You're a free agent.' It was good to put the reminder out there, for her own benefit more than Kate's. Even as she said it, she knew it sounded more like a challenge than a warning. A statement she wanted Kate to deny.

Kate didn't rise to the bait. Instead, she just cocked her head to one side slightly, as if amused. 'If I want to write a really good article, then I have to give more than just my opinion. People want to know the background story, especially when something is promoted as a more humane alternative. There have been lots of scams over the years. So yes, I like to get a good story from those involved.'

'And did you?'

'Yes. I think so. When it comes to tourists, most people want to cut corners and make a quick buck.'

'I think trying to get twenty people on a boat this size is cutting corners.'

'I agree. That was why I asked her about it. Twenty is the legal allowance. Peppi told me they never plan to take more than fifteen.'

'Peppi huh?' Hayley couldn't help but tease again. 'Do you get on first name terms with everyone you meet?'

'Only the interesting ones, *Hayley*.' The jibe came straight back and Hayley couldn't help but laugh.

'Okay, you win. Anything else interesting that we didn't get during the spiel at the beginning?'

'Other than this is her uncle's boat and he's been spotting dolphins for forty years. He's a fisherman by trade and he's been going out into these waters since he was a boy.'

'It all sounds very romantic.'

'That's what sells the story. Anyway, he knows how the dolphins in these waters behave. He doesn't believe in using technology to track them down. He prefers to use his experience. Honestly, I think he wouldn't know how to use it if he wanted to, but that doesn't matter I guess. Peppi has been going out on the water with him and her father since she was a little girl. She wasn't as into the fishing side of things as they were though.'

'If you write your article in the way you've just told it to me, then perhaps you might actually have a shot at convincing people to take this option over the other ones.'

'Do you really think so?'

'I do. It's got a feel-good vibe to it. When people are planning holidays, they want to feel good.'

'Exactly. Besides, it really is the right thing to do. I mean, look at the size of this boat. Back in Cairns, I've seen catamarans carry four hundred people over the Great Barrier Reef, destroying it in the process. All in the name of making the highest profit per head count. If I can show people there are alternatives, better options, then I will.'

'Does your recommendation depend on whether or not we actually see any dolphins?'

'I'm not going to lie, it would help. I have three criteria that need to be satisfied.' Kate had returned to serious work mode. Hayley couldn't help but find it attractive.

'And they are?'

'Firstly, the dolphins. Like you say, they really are a big part of a dolphin watching trip. Can't pretend otherwise. Secondly, the food. If the food is good, then that can be a selling point in itself. The bigger operators offer plenty of free booze, but it's crappy quality. If the food is good and traditionally Spanish, then it adds to the authenticity of the local experience.'

'You could be one of those sales girls who cons people into going on these trips.'

'I'm not sure if that's a compliment or not.'

'Neither am I,' mused Hayley. Regardless, she was riveted by the words coming out of Kate's mouth. Or was she just entranced by the way her lips moved? She cleared her throat and forced herself to focus. 'And what was the third thing?'

'Peppi.'

'Excuse me?' Hayley almost choked on the thought.

'She has to be engaging. Interesting. Don't get me wrong, she's been great to chat to this morning. But that was just one-on-one and I was doing most of the talking. When we get further out to sea, she has to make the journey exciting. That's a real skill.'

'A skill? Isn't that stretching it a bit?'

'Think about it. Look around you. Being on a boat trip is nothing like being a conventional tour guide in a city. There are no landmarks to refer to. No trees or historical buildings. You have blue sky above and blue sea all around. That's pretty damn hard to make interesting if the dolphins decide not to come out and play. Water, water, more water.' She shrugged and Hayley knew she had a point. It was easy for her to be happy just looking at Kate, but for other people, they wouldn't have quite the same requirements.

'How's she doing so far?'

'Only a five out of ten. Maybe a six. But you can bet I'll be keeping my eye on her.' Kate gave the side of her nose a playful tap. 'I'm a ruthless investigator when it comes to these things.'

'I'm sure you are.'

As if on cue, Peppi poked her head out of the downstairs area where she had been hiding away and clapped her hands together to get their attention. 'Everybody, the food is ready downstairs. Do not worry about missing the dolphins. If any appear, the captain will let me know and we can return to the deck. There are also viewing windows downstairs for your pleasure.' She then repeated the message in German and Spanish, even though Hayley was sure that Peppi and her uncle were the only actual Spaniards onboard.

When Kate stood up and held out her hand, Hayley took it, allowing herself to be pulled up. It felt like a familiar, intimate gesture, and one that lasted for a fraction too long once she was already on her feet.

Hayley steadied herself against the movement of the boat, something made more difficult by the weakening of her knees that came with Kate's touch. She followed her into the saloon and wondered if Peppi would meet with the required standard to jump the score from her current five-maybe-six ranking.

She knew Kate would be assessing food for flavour and apparent quality. She, on the other hand, was assessing it for tricks of the trade. She knew all about how to make pre-packaged food appear homemade. It had been an early tactic back when she was learning the ropes and doing everything in a single day was beyond her reach. Hotels in the area watered down the drinks to make the alcohol last longer, masking the lack of spirits with sweet syrups instead. It was done everywhere, but Kate had sold her on the promise of something more from this tour. It had to stand out above the competition.

Kate's plate was already full. How did that girl stay in shape when she ate so much and sat in front of her computer all day?

She nodded when Kate gestured to a table with a great window view and walked over. She put her plate down and then snagged them both a drink while Hayley continued to fill her plate.

'Cheers' Kate said, raising her glass once they were both seated.

'What are we toasting to?'

'To a nice day,' Kate paused for a second. 'And to seeing dolphins. I really hope we do.'

'Me too,' replied Hayley, surprised to find that it was true. Despite her general dismissiveness about the whole experience, now they were here she could feel the excitement begin to build.

'But first we need to eat. Take notes. I'll be quizzing you later...'

#

Lunch wasn't quite finished when the boat began to slow and turn. Kate was on her feet, grabbing her hand and moving towards the front of the boat.

'What's the matter?' Hayley asked, as Peppi called up to her uncle. For some reason, panic was her first response. Sudden movement when they were in the middle of the ocean with only miles of water around and below them was not something she particularly felt comfortable with.

'He's spotted something.' She let go of Hayley's hand to brace herself against the sides of the boat with both hands, leaning out over the water. An image of her falling overboard flashed through Hayley's mind, making her move forward against her own volition. Since when had she cared so much? Since when had she wanted to hold someone close and keep them safe? 'There.' Kate pointed across the water and gave her the excuse to push the feelings away. It also gave her the excuse to stand close enough for the anxiety to disappear.

'Where am I - oh,' Hayley's eyes scanned the water and then saw what Kate had spotted just moments before. Three dolphins, moving through the water in perfect harmony, no more than a boats length away from them.

'Aren't they beautiful?' Kate's question was rhetorical, little more than a whisper of wonder. They had been joined by the other tourists now and Peppi explained that the smaller one was a calf, probably less than a year old. The clear turquoise of the ocean shimmered over their bodies as they moved with grace above and below the surface. One took the lead, dipping in and out of the white tips of the waves created by the boat. It played in their slipstream, sometimes just coming to the surface, before breaking away with a power and speed that was mesmerising.

As the captain steered the boat, moving faster again to keep up with them, Peppi disappeared to work the sails, commandeering one of the other couples to help her. 'We're going to do as much as we can under sail,' Kate explained. 'I've seen it before. We get to move faster, but without pushing the engines and making too much noise. Plus, those who get to help really feel like they've had an immersive experience.'

The thrust of the boat made the waves from its sides bigger and Hayley was amazed to see it drew the dolphins closer, rather than scaring them away. Instead, they frolicked and surfed in their wake, fighting the force with sheer muscular strength.

It was as if they knew why they were there and had decided to play along with the humans and their toys. She could finally understand why sailors had always seen them as good luck charms. As friends in the middle of an ocean that was dark and unpredictable.

Hayley decided dolphins were her new favourite

animal. Perhaps it was time to get another tattoo. A design to stand alongside the old one, marking the passage of time. A symbol of the new chapter of happiness in her life. A dolphin felt like freedom.

Don't get too careless, a voice warned her. The freedom she felt could disappear as quickly as the water below could swallow her whole.

Kate stood at her side, one hand holding the rail as the other pointed out another movement in the water to Hayley. Other dolphins from the pod came close or drew away as they stood there. She moved comfortably with the thrust of the boat, at times her whole body pressed against the length of Hayley's as it pushed them together. She wondered if the other passengers thought they were a couple and her cheeks warmed with pleasure at the thought they might. If she was anyone else, if she was a normal person, she would have been thrilled and proud to have people believe that someone as perfect as Kate could be her girlfriend.

She turned her head and smiled at the unabashed joy in Kate's eyes. It cost her nothing to witness this moment. It was two people having a fun day together and that was no sin.

No, the voice warned her again, it wasn't a sin.

Just the start of a slippery slope that led directly to damnation.

#

Hayley checked her watch, surprised by how quickly the time had flown once they'd found the dolphins. They could have watched them for hours. When Peppi had asked if anyone had to get back to the harbour for the time stated on the promotional flyer, it had been a universal no. At that point, the whole thing took on a more informal air. Now, she realised, they were going to be back at least two hours later than she had expected. Time made no sense when she was with Kate, no matter what they were doing.

Peppi served more drinks and the exhausted tourists settled back into their original groups. The wind was cooler now, stronger as they changed direction and headed back inland as the day rounded to a close. Kate pushed their bodies closer together and Hayley didn't move away.

'So,' asked Kate, 'have you had a good day after all?'

'Yes.' Despite her natural inclination to fight and deny it, it felt better just to be honest. Besides, she was still buzzing from the experience. 'It was amazing.'

'It was for me too. I'm really glad you agreed to come with me,'

'Me too. You're very persuasive Miss Lanthorn. And as annoying as it is, I'm also grateful.'

'I know I can come on strong when I believe in something. That's just who I am. I don't regret it in the slightest. This was a great day out. The planet never stops being amazing.'

'I love how you don't have a cynical bone in your body.' Hayley took a sip of her drink. She'd opted to stick with a no alcohol approach. As the temptation of Kate remained strong, she knew it was the right thing to do.

'Is that what you think?'

'Why, do you believe you can be cynical? Because I saw how happy you were earlier. And the other day. In fact, I don't think I've ever seen you anything other than, how can I put it? Relentlessly cheerful.'

'I am a little,' Kate laughed. It was a sound that resonated in Hayley's heart. 'But that doesn't mean I can't be cynical. I am, about a lot of things.'

'Such as?'

'Would you believe me if I said relationships?'

'Definitely not.' Hayley answered immediately. It was clear Kate had pursued this thing - whatever it was - between them, in a relentless way. She was playing the long game, despite her transient status. She had not been sceptical about the possibility of them having a relationship, Hayley was sure of that.

'Well, you're wrong. I don't trust people easily. I try to do things regardless, otherwise I would still be back in Australia living a safe life. I take moderate risks. But when it comes to other people, especially romantically, I don't give my heart away.' In the dusk, it sounded like a confession.

'Ever?'

'Not for a long time.' Kate gave a slightly wistful smile and Hayley knew then she was telling the truth. The surface of openness and her outgoing nature made Kate appear unguarded. It was easy to assume that extended to every area of life, not just the plants and creatures she was so passionate about. 'Not since I left home.'

'Not even a casual relationship?' Hayley looked out over the waves, glad her sunglasses hid her eyes.

'Definitely not one of those. People think that they're an alternative to settling down, but they've never felt that way for me. Sorry to disappoint you.'

'You don't disappoint me. I'm just surprised, that's all. I know what you've said before. It's just…hard to imagine a girl like you hasn't been inundated with offers. It takes a lot of willpower to say no all the time.'

'You'd think so, but no, not really. It's easy to say no. You must do the same.'

'The only offers I get are from the other side of the bar and there's usually alcohol involved. Lots of alcohol. It's nearly always men. So any propositions in my life are easy nos.'

'Until I came along?' It wasn't cocky or arrogant. Just a simple acknowledgement of the night they had spent together.

'Until you came along,' Hayley nodded with a nervous swallow.

'You were my first easy yes too, if that makes you feel any better. And the only reason you don't get more offers is because you hide yourself behind that bar all the time. Where it's safe.'

'You don't know me,' it was a half-hearted denial, because every word Kate said was true and they both knew it.

'I think I do. I'd love to know who broke your heart so badly that it made you feel that way.'

'What makes you so sure that it was a broken heart?' Hayley was surprised by the assumption. She'd never mentioned anyone else, no previous loves.

'Why else do people start a brand new life in a different country and refuse to date people?' On that point, it turned out, Kate was wrong, but to correct her meant providing a truthful alternative. That, Hayley knew, would open Pandora's Box. It was better to agree, without telling another lie.

'Let's just say that I decided a long time ago that I would never let myself get hurt again.' Hayley decided that sounded like she agreed with Kate's assumption, without having to explain further. She wished she could tell her the truth. Not absolutely everything, of course, but they were good together. They were having a good time. Now, as the sun began to set and the breeze became cooler, it felt instinctive and right to press their bodies together to protect against the chill of the evening air. Kate deserved better than she could give her. 'And you are right. Behind the bar feels a safer place to be.'

'Even today?'

'Especially today.' Hayley turned to look at Kate. 'I've really enjoyed myself with you. Again. You make me want to forget about the bar. I'm doing things that I've never done before and it feels good.'

'But?'

'But we both know that spending too much time with someone else, getting close to them, is the exact opposite way to avoid a broken heart.'

'I'm sorry if I've pushed too hard.'

'You haven't. This has been perfect. That just makes it harder.'

'I know.' Kate reached down and slid her hand into hers. 'But each morning I get up and it's you I want to spend the day with. I'm not expecting anything in return, but I can't help the way I feel. I don't even understand it. But being with you, having fun, it just feels right.'

'I wish it didn't.' It was a hurtful thing to say but the words were out before Hayley could stop them. She held her breath, hoping that she hadn't offended or upset Kate.

'Me too,' came the soft, sad reply.

CHAPTER TWELVE

'What time is it there anyway?' the voice in her ear asked and Kate checked her watch.

'8am,' she replied, tucking the phone under her chin. She was the one who had instigated the call and had hoped that, given Thailand was five hours ahead, Sophie would be awake.

'You never change do you? I've just woken up. Heading down to the beach for the afternoon. You work too hard.'

'It's not work if you love it,' Kate shot back. Out of all the people she had met during her travels, Sophie was the one she stayed in touch with. The two of them were exact opposites, but that was part of the fun. She had been Kate's connection to the fun side of life for a few years. Now she was her connection to the other side of the world and the life she had - temporarily - left behind.

'Well in that case we'd better make hanging at the beach a job, because that's the only thing I'm loving right now. How's *Espania*?'

'Nice. Europe is completely different to Asia. I think I like it.'

'You don't sound convinced?' There was a muffled swearing and Kate didn't even want to know what Sophie was up to.

'Sorry, other things on my mind,' Kate said. She'd wanted to speak to Sophie but now she had her on the phone, she wasn't sure what to say.

At that time of the morning, only Pablo was awake and moving around. She'd taken Hayley's advice days ago and purchased a secret stash of coffee to hide in her room. She'd offered him a cup when the two of them had passed in the kitchen and chuckled when she saw he had his own.

He'd disappeared back to his room and now she was out on the veranda alone. She sat in an old battered chair he'd left out there, looking out over the hill and down to the ocean. What could she even tell Sophie? The other girl knew all about her no hook-ups policy. Even the hint of romance and she would find herself on the other end of an interrogation, even down a long distance call.

'What's up Kate? Are you in trouble?' genuine concern filled Sophie's voice and for all her flakiness, Kate knew that she was lucky to have her as a friend. If she were in trouble, then Sophie would always be there to bail her out.

'No, I'm not in trouble. I promise.'

'Then what is it? When are you coming back?'

'That's the hard part.'

'You like Europe that much huh?'

'Maybe. I don't know. I haven't exactly seen much of it. Just London and here.'

'Not enough to make a decision girl.'

'I thought when you saw Koh Lanta for the first time you decided you'd found your island home?'

'That's different. I just wanted somewhere pretty and tropical to settle down and top up my tan. I don't have the wanderlust that you guys seem to have.' It was true. Sophie's parents were rich and her 'online business' was little more than a facade. She was slumming it on the island as far as they were concerned, even though she was staying in one of the nicest apartments available. She'd arrived, partied hard and never left.

In some ways, Kate saw her as a second home. A place she could always return to. In just a few years, she'd been a more constant presence than her actual home. Her parents were people to contact out of duty, to let them know she was still alive and no, she wasn't coming back any time soon. Her Uni friends had all drifted away. Sophie, with her no ties lifestyle, was somehow her biggest anchor.

'So what's on your mind?' Sophie asked and Kate wondered if she should tell her. She had always been pushing Kate to have fun, to have some casual affairs. To start living again, as she put it. Kate had no intention of living the same way as Sophie, but the merest hint of a potential love affair and Sophie would push her to go for it without needing any further information.

'I'm just trying to work out where to go next.'

'See, I told you. The wanderlust strikes again.'

'Actually, not so much.' This time, there was no hiding the hesitation.

'Wow. That place must have got under your skin. What's so special about it?'

'I don't know if I can describe it.' It wasn't that she couldn't find the words to paint a picture of the hillside falling away to the ocean beneath her. Or the way that the water started out as a brilliant turquoise close to the white sand and transcended to midnight blue as it moved away from the shore. Those were images Sophie could see for herself, even as they spoke. The air might be soaked with humidity over there, while she was basking in the dry heat blowing over from the Sahara, but that was the only difference. 'It's a pretty place. Not the most beautiful I've ever seen and there isn't a hell of a lot going on over here.'

'You're not selling it to me honey.'

'I'm not trying to. There's not enough going on here to keep you busy for a week, let alone a lifetime.'

'You need to book a flight back then, because I'm not coming to visit you. I might make the journey for Paris. Or Milan. But not playa del boring.'

'It's not that bad.'

'Next you'll be telling me that there isn't a bar.'

'Oh, there's a bar,' Kate smiled. She couldn't help herself. What the hell. She couldn't keep skirting the issue. 'One with a cute barmaid.'

'Well, well, well. It only took moving to Europe for you to remember you're a woman. A woman with needs. Needs which, I'm assuming, this barmaid has managed to fulfil?'

'Ewww.'

'Don't ewww me. I want details. The gorier the better.'

'You are truly gross with no sense of boundaries, have I ever told you that?'

'You have, but not often enough to change me. So

spill. Tell me about her.'

'Well, she's not really a barmaid. She does work behind the bar, but she actually owns the place.'

'Wow. That sounds grown up. Let me guess. Older woman?'

'Yes.'

'How old?'

'Thirty six, I think.'

'Please tell me she looks like Lil from Coyote Ugly. I'd fly over there to see that.'

'Now you mention it,' Kate couldn't help but tease. That kind of tub thumping bar was Sophie's idea of heaven and, she suspected, Hayley's idea of hell. 'Don't worry, she's not quite so hard as nails. But close.'

'So how long have you been seeing her? Is this a serious thing?'

'We're not seeing each other.'

'Wait a minute. Not only have you finally hooked up with someone after so long you might as well be a virgin again, you've been having a no strings attached fling?'

'No!'

'Oh I see.' The tone at the other end of the line became ominous. 'Nothing has happened at all has it? We're having a conversation about an attractive woman that you have only actually laid in your imagination.'

'No, I promise. It was most definitely real. It happened the night I arrived. And it was amazing.' Kate checked over her shoulder to make sure that no one could hear, the grin spreading over her face. It felt so strange to actually be able to talk about what had happened.

'Ok, now that sounds more promising. Seriously, give

me the details.'

'Well, she was here when I arrived and it just felt right the moment I saw her. We were chatting and drinking and, there was just…a connection, you know? Like there was something between us. I hadn't felt that way for such a long time. I thought she was staying here, but it turns out she's actually good friends with the guy who owns the hostel.'

'I wish you weren't staying in a hostel. The thought makes my skin crawl.'

'*That's* what you're taking away from this story?'

'You know what I mean. Carry on.'

'We seemed to be getting on well and I just sort of invited her back to my room and she said yes. And I know it's been a long time for me, but seriously, I think it might have been the best sex of my life.'

'She must be good. Or have you fallen for a player? Is that what this is about? You've ended up having a one night stand without meaning to and now she keeps turning you down?'

'God, I wish you weren't close. But it feels that way.'

'Please. Whatever you do, have a little self-respect. Don't go fawning over her like a lost puppy waiting for scraps when she only has eyes for other women. I expect better from you. Besides,' Sophie added with a flourish, 'treat 'em mean, keep 'em keen.'

'It's not like that. I've been working at the bar loads when she's there. I've turned up unannounced. The closest I've seen to her flirting with other women is when she teased an old lady about her morning cup of tea. She doesn't have eyes for anyone else.'

'Afraid of commitment?'

'I think so.'

'Like you. Fantastic. What a great pair you make.'

'You're not being helpful. Besides, I'm not afraid of commitment. I'm just not interested into going into situations where I already know I'm going to get my heart broken. That is just sensible if you ask me.'

'Which is why I never ask you. You think that body and mind are the same thing. If that was the case, my mind would have been well and truly blown years ago.'

'That is repulsive on so many levels. And also, not helpful. What am I going to do?' Kate groaned and smacked her head with her palm. 'We keep hanging out together because I keep asking her to and she always says no at first then agrees. We're having a great time together. But every time I think we're getting closer, she says something to remind me that she doesn't do relationships and we won't be having a repeat of the night we met.'

'Then you should take her at her word. Stop doing this to yourself. You worry that someone is going to break your heart but this is all about you. You're the one setting yourself up to get hurt. It sounds like this woman, no matter how hot she is, has been completely up front with you about the way she feels. If you carry on chasing her after that, then you're going to cause yourself a world of pain.'

'But I don't believe her.'

'Spoken like a true crazy person.'

'I'm not crazy.'

'Next you'll be trying to justify how you're spending the nights watching her through the window just to make sure she's safe. Crazy talk. Lust makes fools out of all of us honey, you're not the first.'

'You may think I'm crazy, but I know she feels something too. I'm sure of it. I just don't know how to get her to see that I'm genuine.'

'Kate, you're calling me to talk about where you're going to go next. How can she think you're genuine when you've already got one foot out the door?'

'And that's the problem, isn't it? I should be planning my next move and all I can think is that I want to stay here. In this beautiful-but-not-amazing, quiet, nothing to do town. Just to have the chance to spend a few more weeks with her.'

'Lord you have it bad.'

'I know. So what do I do? I can't get her out of my head. When we're together, I just want to look at her. When we're apart, I just want go see her. I'm actually daydreaming about us doing things together and being a real couple. Do you know how insane that is?'

'I believe I made that clear when I called you a crazy person.'

'Yeah,' Kate conceded. 'You're probably right. But it doesn't help me though.'

'Look, there's no reason why you have to move on so soon. Is there?'

'No, I've got nothing else booked. I was thinking of heading over to Lisbon for a few months.'

'Then stay there instead. If you have nothing in the diary, give yourself an extra month. Stay and see where it goes with this woman who has given you the most amazing sex of your life. If in a month she's still saying no and you're still following her around like a lovesick teenager, then you have to get out of there. Make it fast, like pulling off a band-aid. It sounds like it's going to hurt anyway, so make it fast.'

'I wish you weren't right.'

'I have plenty of experience in affairs of the heart. Look how many hot surfer chicks have passed by this island. I see myself as part of the travel experience. You can't have any regrets. But walking away isn't a bad thing if it needs to be done.'

'Thank you.'

'You're welcome. Besides, I miss you. I want you to come back to visit.'

'Soon enough.'

'Not if this mystery woman decides to give in to your charms and get what the rest of us tried and failed to do.'

'You didn't try anything.' Kate laughed and then paused. 'Did you?'

'Oh Kate, you're so oblivious to life sometimes it's perfect. Of course I tried. That first night we met. And the second. Then I gave you up as a lost cause.'

'Wow, that quickly.'

'Some people are meant to just be friends. So, are you going to let me know how it goes? I read the new article by the way. Sounded fab. Super cute dolphins.'

'She was there with me. The big one will be out next week. She came with me there too.'

'Oh god, you're starting to sound like a broken record. I'm going. There's some Pad Thai calling my name and I can see a girl on the beach. She's cute and I don't recognise her. I can't miss an opportunity because I'm playing love guru to the hopeless with you.'

'I'll remember that. Go on then, get the girl.'

'Oh, I will. Talk soon. And Kate,' she paused and Kate knew that despite the light tone the two of them always kept, Sophie was about to be serious. 'Don't let her break your heart when you've only just allowed it to mend. Don't let her, but don't *make* her do it either.'

With that, Sophie hung up. It seemed like an odd way to say goodbye, but Kate knew it had been the final word on the matter.

She put the phone down at her side and stared out over the ocean. The sun was rising fast and with it, the day was turning into another scorcher. The dusty heat caught the back of her throat and she knew she had to do something that wasn't about Hayley. She needed a day of not looking at her to get her head straight.

She'd paid up for a few more days at Pablo's. In her time there, only a handful of other people had turned up and gone again, only staying for a few nights. She was sure her room would still be available if she wanted to extend it.

Perhaps Sophie was right. Stay a month and see what happened.

What would she do here for a month? There were other things she could catch up on, she supposed, boring admin tasks she had been putting off for a quiet time. Perhaps this was finally the chance to work through her to do list.

And if it wasn't?

Then she could go again, she rationalised. With that, the decision was made. There was nothing to tie her down here if she wanted to go. If things carried on the way they were, then she knew she would hit make or break point with Hayley soon.

She didn't know what she was more afraid of. Hayley breaking her heart by saying no, or Hayley finally saying yes and altering the journey her life was taking forever.

CHAPTER THIRTEEN

Hayley slammed the car door and looked at the hostel. It was the first time she had been up to Pablo's during daylight hours for over a week. He'd painted the outside and she had to admit, it was starting to look more like a verified backpackers than a rundown house with a few extra beds for hire.

There was even a sign. An actual sign, not one that Pablo had handwritten himself.

She debated going round the back, but then decided to enter the hostel by the main door, in case there were any other pleasant surprises waiting for her. She guessed the painting must be complete, because he hadn't asked for her help again recently.

The main entrance now had an actual reception. With a bell. That was a nice touch, Hayley thought. She bopped the top of it, listening to how the brass tinkle echoed down the hallway and into the belly of the house. There was a scuffling noise from somewhere and Pablo darted out of a doorway. 'Oh. It is you.'

'Nice to see you too. Or do you only have time for paying customers now? I came to bring you this.' It was a spare wrench she had left over from renovating the bar years ago. She'd promised to give it to him the next time she saw him. Not exactly an urgent delivery.

In fact, it was the flimsiest excuse ever to come up to the hostel, but she hadn't seen Kate for a few days and she couldn't think of a better reason. She hoped that Pablo wouldn't see through her thin disguise.

'Ah, thank you. Yes, I had forgotten. Coffee?

'Si.' Hayley followed him down the corridor and into the communal kitchen area. She was pleased to see that it, too, had finally been finished. It actually looked lived in now. The handwritten fuera de servicio signs had disappeared from the appliances so she assumed they were now properly wired up and ready for use. 'This place is looking great Pablo.'

'Thank you. It has been hard work. You were right, it took many, many days. More than I thought possible.'

'Did Javier fix the tank?'

'Today, we do not talk about Javier.' Pablo gave her a thunderous look and waggled his finger in her face. She took that to mean that Javier had once again lived down to her expectations. She was tempted to push, just for the fun of seeing Pablo get all worked up and animated, but decided better of it. Instead, she looked out of the kitchen window.

Her eyes immediately zoned in on Kate. She was there at one of the picnic benches, her laptop open. A young man sat next to her and Hayley felt her stomach clench as she watched Kate throw her head back and laugh at whatever he had said.

It was probably innocent. She had made it perfectly clear that both of them were free agents and it was meant to stay that way.

She had no right to jealousy. So why did it feel like she was ready to storm out there and rage against the world?

'New guy?' she said, her aim for a casual tone going way off the mark. Pablo looked up and joined her at the window.

'Si. He arrived yesterday.' He stroked his chin for a moment, trying to remember the name. 'Chad.'

'Chad? That's very…American.'

'Si, si. He is from California.' Pablo pronounced it with a long emphasis on the second syllable. 'He does the thing she does,' he waved dismissively in the direction of Kate. Pablo understood the complexities of the millennial job world about as well as she did.

'Is he staying here long?' her jaw was tight. Her hands were scrunched in fists at her sides, the car keys digging into her palm. Hayley knew she should stop asking questions, but somehow couldn't help herself.

'He has paid for the four night special.' Pablo looked confused by her sudden interest in the actual running of business. She was about to stop asking when she saw the penny drop. He looked out again at the two of them sitting at the bench and then back at Hayley. Before she could say anything else, he began to chuckle.

'What?' she said, crossing her arms defensively.

'I see what is going on here.' He grinned. She resisted the urge to stamp her feet in frustration.

'There is nothing going on here.'

'Oh yes. You like her. Very, very much, no?'

'It's not like that. Now are you going to give me that coffee or do I have to go?' He looked at her, almost with pity, she thought, before turning back to the counter and making them both a coffee.

'Do you want to go outside to drink it? We could go sit with them. Or we can sit by the entrance.'

'Let's sit on the veranda.' Hayley made the decision. It was hard enough to know that Kate was having such a good time with someone else. Someone who was definitely more her type. Same age, same hobbies, probably also 'didn't do labels'. She didn't need to go in and break it up. Wasn't this the reason she hadn't wanted to get involved in the first place?

As they returned through the dark hallway to the front of the building, Hayley remembered Kate's words when they had been eating dinner in the park. How she had refused to pin down her sexuality. Perhaps this was exactly what she meant. Hayley had missed her chance and the next opportunity had come along.

Pablo talked about the renovations as she sipped her coffee. She was grateful for her sunglasses so he couldn't see her eyes. He filled her in on the progress of the building but she had only one ear open. Her mind kept going back to Kate - the person she was really here to see – sitting nearby with Chad. She already hated the name.

Was that why she hadn't been around lately? Because she'd found a new toy to play with? Kate had promised her that she would continue to show her new things, to continue to surprise her.

Well this had been the biggest surprise of all so far and it hurt like hell.

Hayley put the cup to her lips and tipped it back. Nothing came out and she couldn't remember drinking the last of it. It was empty inside.

Like she was.

Damn, she wanted to hit herself. She had known it would feel this way if she let Kate keep getting closer and closer each time they met. She had only herself to blame and she knew it. Every single warning system she had in place had been going off since the moment the two of them had met and she had ignored all of them. One by one, she had pushed them aside until it was too late and she had…

The words snuck up on her and her hand flew to her mouth. Pablo, pointing at something in the opposite direction didn't notice the sudden move. Hayley let the words tumble around in her brain, unable to find a place to settle, too dangerous for her to process them.

Despite everything, she had fallen for Kate. She knew it now.

She had worried so, so much about hurting her and yet she had ended up with the broken heart first.

Wasn't that the way the universe worked, she thought bitterly? It had been so long since there had been a problem. So long since she had been punished for something. Now, it seemed, this was to be the twentieth anniversary present of her father's sins to pay for.

A punishment she had brought upon herself. 'I've got to go,' she said. Before Pablo could question, she stood up and handed him her empty coffee cup. 'Thanks for the drink.'

'Hayley?' he looked at her and she could see the worry and concern in his eyes. She waited for a second question, but it didn't come.

'I need to get some more work done at the bar. I can't sit out here drinking coffee all day. Come by later though, yes?' It was a peace offering. A lie to pretend she was okay and there was nothing for him to worry about.

'Si.' He nodded, but continued to look at her intently. She knew he would ask her questions when the time was right. For all his buoyant personality, Pablo could tell when it was the wrong time to do something. She would get a reprieve now. He would grill her for answers eventually.

Hayley could feel his eyes on her back as she walked down to the car. She fished the keys out of her pocket and watched as a wet droplet fell onto her knuckle. Damn, she was crying. When did that happen? Tears of self-pity hadn't fallen for years. She wiped them away from her cheek roughly with the back of her hand.

The inside of the car was hot and she waved to Pablo as she pulled away, her thoughts racing faster than she could keep up with. A voice inside was telling her to run. The old fear mechanism, the one that triggered her sense of self-preservation, had come to life again. Kate could be the undoing of her. Hell, Kate already was.

How had she been so stupid? How had she let herself fall so hard for someone who she had known, absolutely known, could never be with her forever? The cracks in her heart hadn't healed at all and now Kate had ripped the paper off and exposed them all over again.

Thoughts of Kate kissing Chad roared into her brain

and she almost swerved off the road at the power of them. She gripped the steering wheel, feeling real, raw emotions take over her body. She had spent a decade comfortably numb and this was too much to bear.

Hayley pulled over and sat with her hands on the steering wheel to stop them shaking. She had fallen in love for the first time in her adult life and it hurt enough to burn her alive.

CHAPTER FOURTEEN

'Hey.' Kate bounced into the bar, barely able to contain her excitement. She had been planning this evening for days and had been frantically hoping that the weather would hold. A rare storm was predicted to blow in tomorrow and she had been terrified it would arrive a day early.

As she'd walked along the oceanfront road towards Hayley's bar, there remained no sign of it. Instead, there were only occasional white wisps of cloud against a deep blue sky. It was the perfect night for a date.

Yes, it was time for date number three.

Kate felt almost giddy. The prospect of surprising Hayley had been made even more poignant by the fact they hadn't seen each other for four days. Not that she was counting, but she totally was. Four days that had felt like a lifetime.

Tonight would, she hoped, satiate the need that Hayley stirred within her. Tonight wasn't part work. There were no excuses for why she needed Hayley's help. Instead, she wanted to give her full time and focus just to them being together. Sure, it had meant spending four solid days working so she could take these next two off and not have to worry about publishing schedules. It had been a godsend to discover Chad at the hostel. He worked remotely as a computer programmer and even though it wasn't quite the same as what she did, he had been able to give her some advice on a couple of new software programmes that had only just come out. He'd helped her install them and it meant that some of the more mundane tasks she could now do in half the time.

This, of course, meant more time available to spend with Hayley.

Speaking of which, the response from behind the bar had been a decidedly distant and formal 'hello'.

'Is everything okay?' Kate asked. Her eyes flicked towards Marco over Hayley's shoulder, but he just shrugged.

'Everything is fine. Can I get you something?'

'Hayley, what's going on?' Kate was upset and concerned. She tried to reach out across the bar but Hayley pulled away like the touch was going to burn. 'Is something wrong?'

'No. I'm just busy.' It was a lie. Kate could tell by the way Hayley looked out towards the empty bar.

'No you're not. Talk to me. Did I do something wrong?' Kate felt her heart drop. She'd spent the four days apart feeling the slow heat of anticipation build. It had never crossed her mind that Hayley might be feeling the exact opposite during their days away from each other.

'I don't know, did you?' The words were harsh and Kate could see that Hayley hadn't intended to say anything at all. Something had happened, something bad, but Kate had no idea what. It seemed though, that Hayley thought she had done something very, very bad.

'Come here,' Kate waved her arm and walked to the far end of the bar, away from Marco and the handful of other customers. For a second Hayley hesitated and Kate hoped she wasn't going to be stubborn. Whatever was going on, whatever it was that she had done wrong, she needed Hayley to tell her so she could put it right.

Kate wasn't ready for this thing to be over. It hadn't even begun.

She held her breath. After what looked like an eye roll of frustration, Hayley joined her. 'Look, I told you I'm busy. Can't we just leave it at that?'

'No we can't. Because you're not okay and you're not busy. If I've done something wrong, then I need to know about it so I can put it right. I thought things were good between us? Is it because I haven't been down here? I've been busy working. I've had so much to do.'

'Oh, I know. I saw how busy you were.' The sarcastic tone cut like a knife.

'What?' Kate was confused. She wanted Hayley to clear things up, not make them more bewildering. 'How busy I was?'

'Yes. I came to Pablo's. To see you.'

'I've been there. I didn't see you. I certainly haven't been anywhere else, if that's what you're implying.'

'You were there. It didn't look like you were busy though. Or working, for that matter.'

'Hayley, stop talking in riddles.' Kate didn't have the time or inclination for games. 'I need to know why you're mad at me. I'm sorry if I haven't been here. I was going to surprise you tonight and it would all make sense, but I have no idea why you're being like this.'

'Look, it's me that has the problem, okay? We can both agree on that. I know you said you weren't into labels and I said I wasn't into dating, so it's not like this is any great surprise. It's just made me realise that we have to stop pretending otherwise.'

'Labels? What's that got to do with anything?'

'You were making it clear you weren't into being exclusive or anything, right? I was just too out of touch to get the meaning. If Chad's your type of thing then great, but don't expect me to be a part of it.'

'Wait? What?' Kate grew even more confused. Was she being accused of cheating? After the pain of what she had gone through with Kazue, then that was the last thing she would ever do with someone. Of course, Hayley didn't know about Kazue and she seemed to have the wrong end of the stick about something. 'What has Chad got to do with anything?'

'I saw you, ok? When I came up to Pablo's. You were all leaning against him, laughing at something on his laptop. You were clearly having a great time. The two of you looked pretty cosy together.'

'This is insane.' Kate felt relief at the easy mix up, and slight concern that Hayley had a taste for paranoia. 'You might enjoy keeping everyone at arm's length, but I don't.'

'Apparently not.'

'Don't be like that. Chad's a really nice guy and yes,

we've spent some time working together the past few days. It's been nice to have someone to share that with. Everyone else at the hostel is travelling, not working. I haven't had those kinds of conversations since I came to Europe. It was nice. He was nice. And helpful. But that's it.'

'So you sit that close to everyone?'

'Have you ever tried to look at someone else's laptop in the sun?'

'No.'

'Then try it sometime. Trust me, it's not easy. Chad and I weren't snuggled up close, or whatever crazy thing you think you saw. Absolutely nothing has happened between the two of us. It never even crossed my mind.'

'And you expect me to just take your word for that?' Hayley was still being defiant, but Kate could see hope in her eyes. She wanted to be wrong. Whatever mixed up thing had happened to her in the past that made it difficult to trust people was going to take more than three dates to crack through, Kate realised.

'Yes. You're going to have to trust me.' Kate reached out over the bar. She took Hayley's hand and this time, she didn't pull away. 'I know this thing between us is something that neither of us were looking for. But I promise you, I haven't even looked at anyone else since the night I met you. Chad is a great guy, but he's not my type. He's been helping me so that I can make sure I give my full attention to you tonight.'

'Tonight?'

'Yes, tonight. And let me tell you, this is not how it was supposed to go.'

'I don't understand.'

'I'd got a special dinner planned for us. Tonight. I spoke to Marco and - don't be mad at him, I know you're the boss - arranged for you to have the night off. So we could spend it together.'

'You did…' Hayley trailed off, stilled by the sudden turn of events.

'I did.' Kate nodded emphatically. She had expected convincing Hayley to take the night off would be a tough sell. She'd known she'd have to finesse the situation when she turned up at the bar. But she hadn't anticipated this battle. 'Please. Don't fight me on this. I want to have an amazing evening with you. You don't have to do a thing other than come with me.'

'But I-'

'And if,' Kate interrupted, 'by the end of the evening I haven't been able to convince you that you're the only one I'm interested in, I promise I'll leave you alone.' It was a huge gamble and a promise Kate didn't want to have to make. The consequences were too great if she couldn't win Hayley round. It was the only thing she could think of to get Hayley to come with her.

'I don't even know where we're going,' Hayley said, looking down at her clothing. She was wearing shorts and a t-shirt that had been a freebie from a beer company.

'Go upstairs and get changed then. A nice pair of jeans, if you want. Something that doesn't make it look like you're doing free booze marketing,' Kate pointed at the t-shirt. 'But it doesn't have to be too fancy.'

Kate watched as Hayley stood on tiptoes to peer over the bar to see what she was wearing. She'd opted for some cream linen trousers and a sleeveless blouse, the one outfit that constituted her 'going out' wardrobe. The majority of clothes in her backpack were chosen for comfort and hot weather, not dating. It was just practical. She had only one nice outfit and tonight she had decided to impress Hayley with it.

Of course, when she had planned this, she had imagined Hayley would notice the change straight away, not be too pissed off to even look at her. Now she was looking and despite her initial hesitation, Kate could tell that she liked what she saw. 'Oh. Okay.'

'But whatever you feel comfortable in,' Kate was quick to reassure her. This was meant to be a wonderful date together and given the less than auspicious start, she didn't want to put any more pressure on Hayley than absolutely necessary. That being said, Kate looked at her watch. 'You've got about fifteen minutes. I'll wait here.' She sat down at one of the few stools that lined the bar.

'Marco,' said Hayley, wiping her hands down the front of her shorts. 'Get Kate a drink.'

'*Sí*,' he said with a polite smile. When Hayley turned away, he gave Kate a huge grin and a double thumbs up.

'I'll be right back,' Hayley said. A look of hesitation crossed her face and Kate hoped she wouldn't change her mind again now. Whatever she was about to say remained unsaid however, and she disappeared behind the bar and up to the apartment above.

Kate finally allowed herself a moment to breathe. So far, nothing had gone according to her plan, but that was okay. There was still time to turn this thing around. She'd had high hopes for the evening and she wasn't going to let a misunderstanding about Chad get in the way.

'Your drink,' said Marco, placing a glass down in front of her.

'I, um,' Kate had been expecting him to ask what she wanted, not make the decision for her. Certainly not one in a highball glass stacked with ice. 'What is it?'

'My house special. It gives courage. Before big date,' he grinned, showing his pearly white teeth. She realised why any young girls on holiday here fell for his charms.

'Thank you. I need it,' she confessed, taking her first sip. It was strong, but not too strong. Dark rum, cola and something else she couldn't quite put her finger on. Before she could ask what it was, he left to serve someone at the other end of the bar.

Kate knew better than to drink quickly to calm her nerves. She'd allowed Hayley fifteen minutes to get ready, but it felt like an eternity sitting there waiting. She hoped she hadn't misjudged anything else.

Then Hayley appeared in the doorway and Kate inhaled, nearly choking on her drink in the process. Between DIY at Pablo's and the bar work, the only time she had seen Hayley's hair loose from its ponytail was the night they had spent together. Even then, it had been in the moments before she had drifted off to sleep.

With her hair falling around her shoulders, Hayley looked softer somehow. Not more innocent exactly, but less like she was guarding herself against the world outside. Kate wondered how long it had been since she'd done something like this. Given the awkwardness of her stance, she guessed a long time. It was as though she was waiting for approval.

Kate nodded, then realised she needed to be honest. 'You look amazing.'

'Not really,' Hayley brushed the compliment away, but not before Kate caught the smile of relief. 'Is this okay though? Not too much?' she looked down at the soft, dusky pink blouse and jeans that left nothing to the imagination about the toned legs underneath. A pair of low heels added the final touch.

'It's perfect.' Kate smiled her most reassuring smile. She kept her desire in check, not wanting to make Hayley more skittish than she already was. 'Now, are you ready to go?'

'I think so. And Marco is happy with this?'

'Yes. Help is arriving in half an hour. There's nothing to worry about. You can just enjoy this evening. I promise.'

'You're making a lot of promises tonight.'

'You can judge me at the end of the evening about whether they were the right thing to do,' Kate waited patiently as Hayley joined her on the other side of the bar.

'You haven't even told me where we're going.'

'I've booked us a table at Mauricio's.'

'I've never been there. Are you sure?' Hayley looked horrified and Kate could guess why. In the next town along, built on the marina, it was popular with higher end holidaymakers and those who moored their yachts. It was edging towards exclusive and certainly the most expensive place Kate had been to in years. Hayley looked down at her outfit.

'I need to go back and change.'

'No. You don't. You look amazing. Jeans are included

in the dress code as long as they're not ripped. I checked.' Kate took Hayley's hand in hers and forced her to stop and look at her. 'I want you to feel comfortable. Tonight I want us to have an amazing time. I don't want it to be fake. I don't want either of us to pretend to be something we're not. So don't worry about what you're wearing. All I want you to do is let me show you how much I like you.'

Before Hayley could say anything else, before she could argue, Kate began walking again. She didn't let Hayley's hand slip from hers as she led them to the taxi that would take them to the real beginning of their third date.

#

'And then,' Kate wound up her story, 'the elephant used its trunk to push him in the water. I know it's wrong to laugh at someone else's misfortune, but he completely deserved it.'

She paused as the waiter reappeared at their table and topped up their wine glasses. The evening breeze rippled the napkin beside her plate and she checked the sky. There was still no sign of the storm as the sun began to set.

Mauricio's sat in a prime position. One side looked out over the marina and the other over a small sandy strip. There they'd set up three tables virtually on the beach itself. It was one of these tables that Kate had selected for their date. So far, only one of the others had been taken, leaving the third strategically empty between them. It had allowed them total privacy so far and once Hayley finished her first glass of wine, they had drifted into easy conversation, her nervousness gone.

Kate hoped the confusion over Chad had been laid to rest. Now that the initial misunderstanding had been laid to rest, she could only hope that Hayley's extreme reaction meant one thing. That she felt strong enough to care about her relationship with Kate. That it was, after all, a relationship rather than just a friendship. They may have gone about it in a strange, back-to-front kind of way, but a relationship was ultimately where they found themselves.

As the waiter walked away, Kate looked up from her wine glass to see Hayley looking back at her. 'Thank you.'

'You don't have to thank me,' Kate said, but her heart warmed regardless. 'I thought it would be nice for us to do something that wasn't an adventure for a change. Somewhere we could just sit and talk, not hike or chase wildlife. Something that wasn't just about my interests.'

'I've enjoyed doing those things with you.'

'I know, but they were *my* things. I was thinking about how I could write about them as we were doing them. Tonight, I don't have to think about any of that. I can give you my full, undivided attention.'

'I think I like the sound of that.' Hayley took a sip of wine, but if she thought it would hide her smile from Kate, then she was very much mistaken.

'Now I realise I've been talking about my travels again so far', Kate smacked her head gently as she said it. 'Which is the exact opposite of making it all about you.'

'Don't be silly. I like listening to your stories. Besides, you know everything I can tell you about my boring little life here. I'd rather hear about your adventures.'

'I wouldn't call them adventures.' Kate knew she was downplaying her experiences. She didn't want Hayley to feel like she was bragging. They were different, that was all. Their lives had taken different paths and that was okay. It had led them towards each other regardless.

'Oh, they're definitely adventures. Painting the bathrooms at Pablo's was the most variation I've had in my routine for a long time.'

'Well I'm glad he managed to convince you to do it. If he hadn't, then we might never have met.'

'True. But don't tell him that. You'll never hear the end of it. Besides, it will give him an excuse to keep asking me to do things for him. I don't have any return favours to ask of him yet. The whole thing could get a little one sided and that is never good for friendship.'

'True. Although I think some of the work his brother did there last week with him wasn't the greatest. I'm not sure it will last until the end of the season.' By which time she was supposed to be long gone, she thought, but didn't add.

'If I know anything about Javier, then I wouldn't expect it to last until the end of the month. I don't know why Pablo ever expects anything different from him, but I guess that's brotherly love for you.'

'I'd probably be the same about my brother,' Kate admitted. 'He's three years older than me, but somehow I was always the responsible one. Always doing my homework and with a sensible career path.'

'That must have been a surprise when you decided to go off into the great unknown and never return.'

'That's an understatement. In the beginning, I think they thought I was just trying to be cool and go walkabout or something. But then when I didn't come back, I think they began to realise that not only was their daughter unlikely to ever bring a nice young man home, there was a chance it would never be her home again.'

'You can't blame them for being surprised.'

'Oh, I don't. I mean, it was hard at first. Really hard. When you've spent so long being the model child, it's a shock for everyone if you decide to spread your wings and go against convention. I think I was annoyed with them for not accepting it all straight away. Distance has been great for helping me to understand where they were coming from, you know?'

'I do.'

'There I go again, talking about me. What about your parents? How did they feel about you leaving England and coming out here?'

'Both my parents are dead.' Hayley said it in a way that didn't invite sympathy. Nor, Kate, realised, did it invite further questioning.

'Oh.' There was a pause while she thought of something else to say. Nothing came. This was awkward. 'I'm sorry.'

'Don't be. You weren't to know. It was a long time ago. I've been on my own for a long time. So when you wonder what made me not want to get into a relationship, it wasn't because I'd had my heart broken. Not in the way you were thinking. It's just because I've been alone for such a long time, I don't know how to do anything else.' Hayley looked away. The admission was one she clearly struggled to make.

'I can see how that would make this seem scary.'

'It's not just scary. I'm not sure I even know how to be in a relationship.' The pain in her voice was upsetting. But, on the bright side, it was also the first time Hayley had admitted a relationship between them was a possibility.

'Don't worry about that now,' Kate reached across the table and took Hayley's hand in hers. She allowed her thumb to stroke back and forwards over her knuckles. It was intended to be comforting, but the soft skin under her own also kindled her desire. 'Tonight is about enjoying ourselves. Not deep and meaningful conversation. That can wait.'

'Thank you.' Hayley looked relieved. As they looked at each other, she didn't pull her hand away.

They sat in a comfortable silence until the waiter came out to serve them. He put two plates of tapas down between them then returned inside to bring out the *pièce de résistance*. A full Serrano ham, on its carving stand. He placed it down heavily on the table and Kate felt her eyes grow wide. It looked amazing.

From his belt he pulled a long thin knife and brandished it towards them with a flourish. He carved the first slice and placed it on Hayley's plate. In a flash, he carved the second and placed it on Kate's. 'Please,' he said, gesturing for them to try.

Kate had grown used to Spanish style food in the few weeks she had been here. Whenever she was at the bar, Hayley had made sure she was well cared for. Pablo had cooked many simple but traditional meals for them in part payment for the inconvenience. Now the work was completed, she realised she missed the amiable community of them.

But this? This was sublime. She had expected it to be chewy, but instead it melted in the mouth. The soft, salty flavours evoked hidden memories and she tried not to groan in pleasure. Instead, she decided to use her words. 'That is amazing.'

'It really is,' Hayley agreed.

'You like?' asked the waiter, but he already knew the answer before Kate gave him the thumbs up. 'Watch,' he said and deftly carved another two slices. He waited for them to finish eating them. 'Now you try.' He gestured to Kate.

'What?' she was horrified.

'You try,' he said again, beckoning for her to stand up. She was tempted to refuse, but knew it was part of the experience. Not only would she get to witness carving at the table, she would get to try it herself.

She watched Hayley suppress a giggle as she pushed back her chair. Her dubious feelings were fully conveyed on her face. She had tried many things before, but they didn't usually involve sharp implements.

As the waiter slowly carved another slice, she watched intently. The knife moved through the meat with precision, taking nothing more than a paper thin slice from the top. How hard could it be? The knife must be sharp enough to make it slide as if through butter.

She held the shank of the ham in her grip for leverage and placed the knife exactly where he had indicated. She took a deep breath and began to move it back and forth.

The knife went nowhere for a few seconds then slid rapidly over the surface of the meat. It glided over the oil leaving her with nothing more than a scrap that had sliced more by luck than judgement. The waiter jumped backwards as the blade carved the air in front of him. Hayley let out a gulp of laughter and Kate glared at her.

'That was my first attempt!'

'I know, I'm sorry.' Hayley did her best serious face and Kate looked at the knife in her hand. She studied the angle of the meat. She could approach it like a scientist. Clearly, she needed to apply a bit more force.

Although, she reasoned, not enough force that she would kill them all in a bloodbath.

She changed the angle of the knife and pushed down, sawing backwards and forwards with all her might. This time, the knife did not slide from her control. Nor, she realised, was it going anywhere at all. She hacked back and forth, until she finally served the triumphant slice to Hayley's plate.

Wafer thin, it was not.

Hayley looked at it dubiously and Kate almost defied her not to eat it. Instead of a translucent, almost salmon pink slice, it was a deep claret red, almost brown at its thickest. As Hayley obliged and began chewing, Kate looked down at the ham. Gone was the smooth, continuous surface that gleamed in the last of the sunlight. Instead, the middle now looked like it had been gnawed ineffectually by a rat. 'Okay, that's enough,' Kate handed the knife back to the water. She knew she could be stubborn at times, but there was no point destroying food for the sake of it. He grinned and deftly rectified her mistakes, slicing them several more cuts, before requesting they enjoy their meal. He disappeared, leaving them alone again as the sun finally set.

Hayley was still chewing on the sacrificial slice. 'It's like jerky when it's thick,' she offered by way of explanation.

'It's harder than it looks to cut that bloody thing.'

'I know. Don't be fooled by the waiters. Or the locals. They've spent years learning how to do it properly. I think you did really well for your first attempt.'

'You're still chewing.'

'When I said jerky, I really meant salty boot leather,' Hayley gulped and swallowed the last of it. 'Don't worry, I'm still going to make sure we enjoy the rest of this though.' She picked up her wine glass and extended it to Kate. 'A toast?'

'Of course.'

'To a wonderful evening.' She clinked their glasses together and Kate couldn't help but smile. This, at last, felt so normal. 'Thank you for bringing me here. For arranging all this.'

'It's my pleasure.'

'I haven't been on a date in years,' Hayley said, putting her glass down and reaching for the food. It was more of an aside and Kate studied her carefully. So much for her belief in dates one and two. She filed away the information that Hayley was a woman who saw wining and dining in expensive restaurants as a couples thing to do.

Trekking, apparently, not so much.

It didn't matter though, thought Kate, as long as she was having a good time. As long as she saw that the two of them could work so perfectly together. Consequences, all the realistic and logical things that held them both back could wait. They had tonight. That was all that mattered.

They shared dessert. The sun had been set for over an hour by the time they finished eating. The sky in front of them was dark. As they drank the last of their wine and talked by the flickering flames of the beach torches set outside the restaurant, Kate watched the lights of an occasional ship blink on and off as it moved along the horizon. She took Hayley's hand in hers as they talked and drank. They sipped slowly and Kate knew that neither of them wanted the night to end.

But, like all good things, she knew it must. As she paid the bill without letting Hayley see the numbers just in case she offered to contribute or, worse, felt she owed her something, Kate felt a strange sense of contentment that she hadn't felt for years. Even in her happiest of moments, when she had taken photos of the most breathtaking landscapes in the world, when she had seen the most majestic creatures, when she had felt truly *alive* - none of those moments had given her this feeling of peace and contentment.

Those feelings came from being close to someone who, right from the start, she had known would upend her plans and carefully ordered world.

As they pulled up outside Hayley's bar, the door was closed and the lights were off. Kate was relieved. There would be no work distractions to pull Hayley back to the real world before she had chance to appreciate how amazing the evening had been. Kate wanted her to lie in bed and just think about the time they had together. That, Kate knew, would be key to getting date number four. She just had to work out what could be better than the things they had done tonight.

Planning could wait for tomorrow. Now, as the taxi meter clicked over, she had to screw up the courage to say goodbye.

'Why don't you come up?' it was so quiet that Kate

almost didn't hear it. In the dark, she could see Hayley's eyes shining with hope and something indefinable. Kate felt her stomach contract. She could barely breathe as the enormity of what Hayley was offering hit her.

'I'd love to,' she whispered, hope and desire flaring like twin flames in her chest.

CHAPTER FIFTEEN

Hayley fumbled as she tried to insert the key in the lock. The anticipation made her fingers weak and the undercurrent of fear added a slight tremble.

She could feel Kate behind her, a hand on her hip, their bodies almost pressed together but not quite. It was familiar and it was arousing at the same time. It was driving her out of her mind.

That, she reasoned as the key finally slid home, was the only explanation for the words coming out of her mouth when she invited Kate in. She had never brought anyone back here. Other than a few delivery men and Pablo, during that one time when there was a problem with the kitchen sink, no one had been up here at all.

From the moment she had laid eyes on Kate, she had been breaking all of her own rules. This, she knew, was the final one. Why hadn't she offered to go back to Kate's room? Had she needed her so badly she couldn't even wait for the drive up the hill?

No, it was more than that, she thought as she offered Kate a drink, autopilot politeness taking over. The hostel felt less real. A temporary place for transient sex. Tonight she wanted to be able to let go in the safety of her own sheets.

It had been so long since she had just allowed herself to be in the moment when it felt so right.

Kate declined the wine, instead closing the distance between them. Hayley watched as she placed her bag on the counter with deliberate care. Now that they were here, now that she had made the bold gesture of invitation, she almost didn't know what to do next. Frozen with not wanting to do the wrong thing, her entire body felt alien to her.

At the first brush of Kate's lips against hers, she realised that the younger woman had no such qualms.

It felt new and like a memory at the same time. Kate kissed her slowly, gently, as if she was trying not to scare her away. Her hand slid up Hayley's bare arm, leaving goosebumps in its wake, despite the heat of the night. The uncontrolled passion of their first encounter simmered under the surface, held in check for now, as it had been every day since. Kate's kisses held the promise of more nights beyond just this one.

They had come too far to turn back now. The carefully created world she'd built from scratch with her own two hands lay at the mercy of the woman whose lips brushed her own.

'I've been dreaming of this since the night we met,' Kate whispered. 'You have no idea how hard it's been, seeing you every day.'

'Yes, I do.'

'I don't think so. If you knew how much I've wanted you, how much I needed you, then you wouldn't have kept yourself away from me. You wouldn't have stopped me from kissing you here,' she moved from Hayley's lips and along the length of her jaw line. She kissed the fluttering pulse at the side of her neck, lips a temporary distraction from the hand sitting on the waistband of Hayley's jeans. 'You wouldn't have stopped me from touching you,' she slid her hand over the thick material, cupping her with enough pressure to dissolve any remaining resolve.

Hayley felt a rush of heat and knew she was ready for Kate's fingers from that single touch. Her body responded to Kate in a way she couldn't understand. All she knew for sure was that she needed to touch as much as she ached to be touched.

'I want to do to you,' Kate continued, 'all the things I didn't get to do that first night.'

'What else is there?' Hayley gasped as Kate slid a thigh between hers, gripping her and pulling them close.

'You'll soon find out.' Kate pulled back and looked in her eyes, voice deep with promise. 'Bedroom?'

'That way.' Hayley pointed at the door and didn't even care what mess might be waiting for them in there. All she knew was that it contained a soft flat surface to press Kate's body against with her own. Nothing else mattered.

She led Kate by the hand, pulling her to a place she had never shared with anyone. The room that had always been her safe escape. Untouched by the outside world and all the danger it contained. Tonight, Kate would break through that invisible barrier and she would let her. It was a permission she swore she would never give, but at the sound of Kate's breathing behind her, all bets were off.

Hands slid into the back pockets of her jeans and squeezed. A simple action, chaste enough in comparison to things to come, but it was enough to send another quiver of desire through Hayley. She spun around, pulling Kate's hands free and placing them around her waist instead. 'I need you so badly,' she confessed. The words sounded alien to her own ears. A shameless pleading.

'Then let me make love to you. I don't want either of us to fight it anymore.' Kate pulled at the button of her jeans, tugging the zip down. 'I want to show you that I'm worth it.'

'You've always been worth it. It's me who's not worthy of you.'

'Shhh,' Kate placed a finger against her lips to silence her. 'None of that. You're the most amazing woman I've ever met. Tonight, I'm going to make you see that.'

Unlike their first night, there was no frantic tearing of clothes. The desire ran as deep, but with a powerful stillness. Hayley let Kate remove each item piece by piece, her body arching towards the mouth that insisted upon exploring every inch as it became exposed. When only her underwear remained, she flipped Kate over and began to do the same, hand sliding under soft cotton to softer skin underneath. When she reached the lace of Kate's underwear, the material was already damp, leaving her with no doubts that Kate's body was as ready for her as she hoped it would be.

She slid the material down over her thighs, cupping a calf in her hand to remove them completely. There was a moment of hesitation, and then she pushed Kate's leg back and to the side, exposing her completely to her view. Kate's breath hitched at being so openly admired, but she didn't pull away. Instead, she allowed Hayley to look at her, glistening in the faint light coming through from the hallway.

'Come here,' Hayley demanded, her voice low and husky in her throat. Kate did as she demanded, straddling her thighs as she sat on the edge of the bed. She braced herself on her knees, her arms around Hayley's neck. Hayley kissed her deeply before turning her mouth's attention to the breasts in front of her, taking first the left, then the right into her mouth. She sucked on Kate's nipples, pulling them into taut peaks as Kate's body began to move in response, her head thrown back to push them harder against Hayley's lips.

Hayley continued licking and sucking as she moved her right hand between Kate's thighs, using her left to hold Kate steady in their precarious position. She moved her fingers back and forth in the soft wetness she found there waiting for her, Kate's body opened for her to explore. The involuntarily shudder at her touch told her that Kate was ready. That she needed her now.

She lined up her fingers, testing and dipping only the tips into Kate. She felt the tension, a reflexive tightening in response to the intrusion, then Kate relaxed. 'Ready?' Hayley whispered. Kate nodded in response, her eyes communicating complete trust.

It was all the invitation she needed. Hayley bent forwards again, her mouth engulfing the nipple that had remained hard and ready, waiting for her. She pushed Kate down with her free arm, bracing her hand for the weight of her body, impaling her on steady fingers in one slick and easy movement. Kate gave a guttural groan of pleasure and pain as she held herself still for a moment or two, her body adjusting to the intrusion. Then she began to rock her hips back and forth, riding Hayley's fingers and rubbing herself against her palm. Hayley's fingers bent and curled with each roll of the hips, unerringly finding the sweet spot that Kate had been waiting for.

She could feel the orgasm building around her fingers, pulling her deeper into Kate's body as she held her closer and tighter. Kate moaned with each stroke and touch, unable to hold back the vocalisation of her desire. She was half-begging, half-sobbing beyond control as she arched into Hayley's hand one final time, her body rigid as the waves of pleasure washed through her and she called out Hayley's name.

Then she slumped against her shoulder, body weak with exhaustion. Hayley lowered her to the bed, words she had never said to anyone playing on her lips but not coming out. She was in awe of Kate's beauty as she lay there, recovering, knowing that her turn would come soon enough.

An hour later, Hayley stared into the darkness, her body heavy with exhaustion. Her hands drifted in delicate circles over Kate's skin, wondering if she would ever stop being amazed by the woman who had come to share her bed. Before the usual darkness of her thoughts could take over, she drifted to sleep with the soft breath of Kate moving in and out in time with her own.

CHAPTER SIXTEEN

Kate's eyes fluttered open and began to adjust to the darkness. There was no temporary confusion, no wondering where she was. Her body was warm with Hayley's pressed against her and the memory of the last few hours together still made her body heavy and sore with satisfaction.

It felt strange - in a good way - being in someone else's room. In someone else's bed. The life she had been living meant that even if she rented an apartment, she always felt temporary in some sense. She had adopted a minimalist lifestyle by necessity. She never had a place that felt truly hers and she never stayed somewhere that was someone else's real home either.

The bed she lay in and the woman it contained were permanent features here. Once, she believed that those kinds of thoughts would frighten her. That they would make her uncomfortable in their familiarity. Kazue's bed had been the last to feel that way and for so long since it had been associated with heartbreak.

This bed felt, in a way she couldn't define, like a home.

Hayley's bar was closer to the ocean than the hostel. There, on the nights when she left out her earplugs and listened for the sound of the waves, they were always distant and inconsistent. Here, in the silence, she could hear them hammer and thud with each roll up the beach. A reassuring thunder that made her want to wake Hayley up with kisses so they could share it together.

Just the thought of kissing Hayley again and what it could turn into ignited a spark of desire that always seemed on the verge of flaring from ember to flame. Her body had never responded so quickly and easily to another woman's touch, not even with Kazue. She squirmed, pressing her thighs together. She was never going to be able to get back to sleep if she continued with those kinds of thoughts.

Perhaps, she wondered, Hayley might actually not be adverse to the idea of being woken up with kisses for another session of mind-blowing sex to the background sounds of the ocean. It didn't sound like a bad proposition when she put it like that.

Apart from being kissed by this mouth, Kate thought when she swallowed. It felt like crap with the after effects of food, wine and…well, it wasn't like she'd had the chance to clean her teeth before passing out from exhaustion. She ran the tip of her tongue over her front teeth, feeling the film. No, it was not the kind of mouth she wanted to be remembered for.

Her eyes could make out the shapes of furniture in the darkness. She slid out of bed, doing her best not to wake Hayley as she moved their bodies apart. Away from hot skin and sheets, her body chilled against the night air, nipples painfully erect from a night of overstimulation. Hayley was going to be the death of her.

Kate made her way from the bedroom to the bathroom. She moved slowly, taking gentle steps, determined not to bump into anything and wake Hayley. No, if she was going to wake her up, it was going to be in the best way possible. The fear of being burglarised was not the emotion she wanted to arouse in the other woman.

Kate shut the bathroom door quietly behind her and groped for the light switch. It was higher than she expected and it took her a few seconds to find it during which a faint sense of panic began to grow. The bathroom had no window; her eyes were unable to find any bearings in the pitch-black room. She flicked the switch and waited a few seconds. The light finally came on and she blinked against the harsh fluorescent glare.

Kate looked at herself in the mirror above the sink. Her mouth was still pink and swollen from so many passionate kisses. Her hair was a tangled mess that told no lies about the things she had done. She ran her fingers through it until they caught in the knots. She would have to spend some serious time with Hayley's conditioner before she left the next morning.

It was too soon to be thinking about leaving. She had no intention of walking out of those doors without another chance to show Hayley exactly how she felt about her. The past few weeks had been the hardest she had ever tried to convince someone she was worth dating, but every single moment of effort had been worth it for the chance to make love to Hayley again.

Kate looked at the toothpaste on the shelf above the sink. Next to it was a solitary toothbrush. Despite everything they had done together, there was something not quite right about going ahead and using someone else's toothbrush the first night you stayed over. She contemplated squeezing the toothpaste onto her finger and using that instead, but the stale taste in her mouth would need something more vigorous.

Hayley probably kept mouthwash somewhere. The mirror above the sink was actually the front of a cabinet, she realised, hooking her fingers under the lip and pulling it open. There, in the middle, was a half-empty bottle of mouthwash. Perfect.

Kate unscrewed the lid and poured a measure out into it. It wasn't a brand she had ever used before. It was soft spearmint flavour, not one of the harsh ones that made everything taste funny for hours afterwards. She decided she liked it. As she moved the liquid around her mouth, she made a mental note of the brand before screwing the lid back on. She put the bottle back on the shelf and continued to swish backwards and forwards. It was very hard to track the required two minutes when you didn't have a watch on because you were stark naked, she decided.

Hands on hips, her eyes darted around the room, taking it in, before settling back on the cupboard in front of her. A small white box caught her eye. The label faced towards her.

Kate didn't mean to look. It crossed all kinds of rules to snoop in someone else's bathroom cupboard. She knew that, but she couldn't help herself. She reached forward and took out the box. It was for diazepam. That explained Hayley's sometimes-overcautious demeanour. Her neutral responses.

Except that, Kate saw with a corresponding hollowness in her stomach, the pills were in someone else's name.

She spat the mouthwash into the sink. It might have been a long time since she'd been intimate with anyone, shared their space, but she knew you didn't keep a stranger's random prescription medication in your cupboard.

The sinking feeling became stronger. Intuition told her she'd found something significant. Kate began to put the pieces into place. The reluctance at getting involved. The reluctance at talking about her life outside running the bar. Not talking about her history. The box was dated only two months ago. It wasn't that old. New enough for there to still be someone else in Hayley's life.

Her whole world, the one she had been building to completion over the past few weeks and had, tonight, felt like a real thing again, began to crumble from beneath her.

Kate swallowed, her newly fresh and minty mouth forgotten. Instead, she put the medication on the sink and turned off the light. She allowed her eyes a few more minutes to get used to the darkness and then opened the door.

Instead of returning to the bedroom, she groped her way along the walls and back to the kitchen. Thankfully, the kitchen blinds were open and the whole room was bathed in shimmering white moonlight. On the counter, she could see the outline of her bag, carelessly tossed there when they came in. She had only been thinking about

Hayley in that moment. Thinking about what it would be like to get her naked and into bed.

Now, the whole memory felt tainted.

She reached into her bag and pulled out her phone. It had automatically connected to the wifi in the bar down below. Pulling up the web browser, she opened a new tab and typed in Rachael Taylor Chapman. She hoped that Hayley's mystery woman was slightly less elusive than Hayley herself was.

Google returned over fifty thousand hits.

As she scanned the first page, the sound of the waves disappeared, replaced by the blood filling her ears. Story after story was displayed. Not the social media sites as she was expecting, but actual news stories. Headlines. Disturbing headlines.

She clicked back to the top of the screen and selected the images function. The face staring back at her was unmistakeable.

It was younger. It was pale and drawn. The hair was a darker shade and the make-up more pronounced. But it was, without a doubt, the woman sleeping in the other room.

Kate's knees gave way and she sank to a crouch. She clasped her hand over her mouth to hold in the gasp of horror as the reality of who she had slept with sank in.

The prospect of there being another woman seemed a much better alternative right at that moment. Instead, all she could see was Hayley's new old name associated with words like killer, murderer, psychopath. The intimation that she knew what her father had done all along was there for anyone who could read between the lines.

Her body racked with silent tears as she tried to process this new information.

Their whole relationship, the one she had fought for with such determination, had been built on nothing but lies. Not the small ones about exes and broken hearts. Not lies by omission. Terrifying, awful lies.

The woman she had finally allowed herself to fall in love with, the woman she had given all of herself to, turned out to be the biggest lie of all.

CHAPTER SEVENTEEN

Hayley woke up with the warmth of the morning sun on her naked skin. The sheet was tangled around her legs, leaving the top half of her body naked and exposed, but she didn't care. It felt luxurious to stretch out and feel every muscle in her body sing.

A contented smile played on her lips. She couldn't hold it in. Nor did she want to. Images from the night before played through her mind in flashbacks. She hadn't slept that well in years. Her sleep had been deep and dreamless. It was amazing, this feeling of happiness.

She rolled her shoulders from the stretch and reached out to the other side of the bed. Kate, if she was lucky, would want a replay of the night before. It seemed impossible not to touch her skin, explore every inch of her again in the light of day.

Hayley's hand stretched out, but came across only more crumpled sheets. She turned and saw she was alone. For a second, she thought it might have been nothing but a dream. The smell of sex on the sheets, undercut with the delicate zesty fragrance of Kate's perfume, told her it was real.

She strained her ears for sounds in the rest of the apartment. She knew Kate was naturally an early riser. Perhaps she had decided to slip off to the kitchen for a cup of coffee. Try as she might, all Hayley could hear was silence. She was more puzzled than worried. Last night had not been like the first night they had spent together, when Hayley had snuck off with her feelings of shame and guilt the morning after. Last night was different enough that she was confident the tables had not been reversed.

The door to the bathroom was open and the light was off, so Kate couldn't be in there. Hayley continued through to the open plan lounge and kitchen, starting to feel conscious of her own nakedness for the first time. It too was empty. She walked over to the French windows and tucked herself behind the curtain to look out. The hope that Kate might have let herself out onto the balcony to enjoy the first of the morning sun disappeared when she saw the empty plastic chair, still covered in a faint dusting of sand. Kate was not sitting there, nor had she that morning.

Hayley drew the curtains back closed and looked around the room. Kate's bag was gone. A sinking feeling ran through her as she walked back to the bedroom where they had so casually discarded clothes the night before. Hers still lay on the floor in a tangled mess. Kate's were missing.

Perhaps, a hopeful, desperate voice from within told her, Kate had left early to get them both breakfast. But surely she would have left a note? Hayley scoured the kitchen for a sign of one, but there was nothing. No indication at all that Kate had ever been there.

The first two tears fell and she brushed them away angrily with the back of her hand. Getting involved with people was dangerous. How had she let herself get in a position where her heart could break like this?

She walked back to the bedroom and threw on a pair of shorts and an old vest top. There was no point looking her best. There was no point making an effort. If last night had been worth it, if she had been worth it, then Kate would still be here.

Coffee seemed the logical way forward. Food was out of the question. As she waited for it to filter through, she turned the events of the previous evening over and over in her head. Each look. Each touch. Every word that had passed between them. She replayed it in minute detail, looking for the moment when she had done something wrong.

But there was nothing.

Try as she might, she simply couldn't see what she had done. When they had drifted off to sleep in each other's arms, Kate had looked as happy as she had felt. There wasn't a look in her eyes that warned she was getting ready to flee. There was nothing to say that now she had completed some elaborate scheme to finally get her own way, that would be enough and she would be gone for good.

Eventually, as she made herself some toast, the tears fell harder and she didn't try to stop them. She had drunk that first cup of coffee slowly, giving Kate time to return with breakfast and for it all to be a misunderstanding. She hadn't walked through the door. Hayley knew every coffee shop and store serving breakfast in a five-mile radius. If Kate was coming back, it would have happened by now.

She forced the toast down her throat, even though she felt sick, not hungry. It tasted like dust in her mouth and swallowing was made harder through the sobbing tears. She had been a fool and now she was paying the price.

She took a bite out of the second slice and put it back on the plate. It was too difficult to keep eating. How was she going to face the day ahead? How, after reaching the highs of last night, could she get dressed and head down to work as if nothing had even happened? Marco was working the lunch shift and she knew if he didn't question her outright, then he would do so with his eyes. The shame of her failings as a woman were too much to bear.

She had given her all. In the end, it still hadn't been enough.

Numb, she threw the remains of toast away and placed the used plate in the sink. She would wash up later. Normally fastidious about keeping the small apartment clean, instead she was filled with apathy. There was no point in keeping a tidy house if she couldn't fundamentally keep anyone else in it.

Another retch of tears and she walked through the bathroom. She was loathe to wash the smell of Kate off her skin, knowing now she would never feel it again. Each movement of her body was a reminder of what they had shared and with each passing second, the reminder became more painful. She flicked on the light and began to remove her top while it stuttered into life.

Hayley froze mid-movement, her arms in the air. Through the gap in the material, she failed to see her reflection.

The cabinet door was open.

She yanked her top the rest of the way off, her eyes seeing the box of medication before anything else. Her brain tied all the pieces together in less than a second. No, no, no, no.

No.

A frantic fear clawed up her throat and the devastation of a broken heart was swept aside in the sudden panic.

Kate knew. She knew.

The thought ran around her brain, bashing itself against the sides and not letting anything else in. For what felt like minutes although may only have been seconds, Hayley was paralysed. She had lived this moment over and over in her nightmares. The ever-watchful sense she had carried with her for years, had finally let her down. She had let her guard drop and walked herself into a trap of her own making for the sake of one night in the arms of another woman.

A woman who she thought she loved, but who would never love her back now.

That, Hayley knew, was the least of her problems. She looked around the room, thoughts of a shower gone. In its place, she did a quick inventory, scanning for the possessions she would take with her and the ones she could leave behind.

She had experienced heaven and it had led her straight into hell.

The act of planning to flee kicked her brain from its

foetal state and into life. She ran to the bedroom and grabbed her bra from the floor. She pulled the tank top back on, the fact it didn't match her shorts not even a consideration.

She had to move. Kate knew, but Hayley didn't know for how long this information had been sitting out there. Had she had the chance to tell anyone yet? If Hayley could just get to her first, it might be okay.

If Hayley could just silence her before she had chance to tell anyone.

The words echoed her father's confessions and she retched, the half-digested toast getting stuck at the back of her throat. She made it to the bathroom and threw up, forcing it out so she could get her feet moving.

It didn't matter now what memories she carried with her. Her only option was to find Kate and try to explain. There had to be a way to make Kate promise she wouldn't tell anyone. Not anyone in the town that had become her home. Not one of Kate's friends or family in a far-off location who didn't know what the revelation of this secret would do to her. The clock ticking towards the twenty year anniversary of her father's conviction meant that she was about to become a public commodity again.

Hayley desperately wanted to believe that Kate wouldn't see her that way. Even if her pleading fell on deaf ears, then there was a chance that Kate would seek revenge for being duped. She wouldn't know, couldn't understand the hell that Hayley had gone through for those years. What damage it would do if she sold her location and new identity to fund the next few years of travels. It made Hayley sick to think about it, but how well did she know

Kate, really? It had only been a few weeks and that wasn't long enough to guarantee that someone could be trusted with your life.

As Hayley grabbed her keys and headed out the door, all her biggest fears surrounded her and filled her head. They crashed around her like a wave and she knew that she could drown in them. It was that same helpless sensation that had made her life a living hell until she managed to escape it the first time.

She left her apartment, hollowed by the sensation that she wouldn't survive it twice.

CHAPTER EIGHTEEN

Chad had loaned her his motorbike without question. A vesper he had hired from the city, it wasn't her usual mode of transport, but that didn't matter right now. He had taken one look at Kate's tearstained face and offered to drive her to wherever she wanted to go. He had stood in the doorway of his hostel room in his shorts and reached out for her.

When she flinched away, he had just nodded and retrieved the keys from his bag. He handed her the helmet, far too big, but better than nothing, and told her to take as long as she needed. She could see him scanning her body for signs of a fight, signs of trauma, but she knew there was nothing. The only physical pain she felt was entirely self-inflicted and she had revelled in every moment of it.

The emotional pain dwarfed it in comparison.

She'd driven like a fool but she didn't care. The roads had been quiet in the early morning. Even the commuter traffic was nothing in the town and the only vehicles on the road that led to the next city along were big trucks and hotel transfer coaches. The occasional car honked its horn at her but she ignored it, weaving in and out of the traffic as she had learned to do in Phuket.

Kate drove with no intentions, but when she arrived at her destination, it seemed logical that she had been aiming for here all along. The gate to the Parque Natural Granadilla was once again locked, but that would not stand in her way. In her shorts and with only a carelessly filled backpack, she had climbed over in no time and dropped to the ground the other side. Inside the perimeter fence, she felt safe. The park was huge and no one would find her there.

Right now, Kate really didn't want to be found.

She couldn't face Pablo. Did he know his best friend was actually someone else? How had Hayley, sorry, Rachael, been able to lie to all of them so smoothly about who she really was? How many other women had she lured into her bed with the playing-hard-to-get attitude?

Was it a cunning and deceptive trick she had learned from her father?

The anger, the fear and something else, harder to name that almost felt like disgust mixed with shame, rose up in her again. Just thinking about Hayley made her furious. Then she would think back to the night before. Every touch had felt so real. So honest. How could that be when everything else between them had been a lie?

Her shins caught on the long sharp grass, tearing at the skin. Stomping through the tears, she had veered off the narrow path and into the scrubland. She blindly course-corrected, the pain of the cuts almost a physical exorcising of the pain she was feeling inside.

Last night, with Hayley's hands on her, inside her, she had almost said the words. They had been about to leave her mouth when an orgasm, the last of many, had crashed over her and took them from her mouth with a gasp. But she had felt them. She had been willing to say them.

I love you.

Were any other words so dangerous?

She hadn't said it, but that would never undo the fact she had felt it. The connection between them had been strung like a wire, throbbing and humming alive in the night. Now, in the light of day, those feelings were battered by darker ones, but they had left her. They had not disappeared when she had seen Hayley staring back from her phone, her face captioned by a single word: evil.

The woman she knew didn't seem evil. Didn't feel like the person she had read about in the darkness before her legs had found the strength to get her the hell out of there and into the cool, pre-dusk air. She had walked to Pablo's in her bare feet, not feeling the gravel underneath as she continued to delve into the digital archives. The cost of a data connection seemed a laughably insignificant concern. Halfway up the hill, the pain had numbed enough for her to approach each click like a research article; a necessary act to discover more about her subject.

Perhaps that, she thought as she pulled a bottle of water from her bag and allowed her feet to stop their incessant marching from the mess she had found herself in, had been her fatal mistake. She had left without asking Hayley to explain. Without demanding to know what the hell was going on.

Instead, she had read her way through the news and out of date sensationalism. The picture it had painted was more bad than good. Instead of hearing Hayley out, she had been left with the impressions of others. Could they be wrong?

She desperately wished they could be. That the woman she knew now was the real one. But wasn't that the mark of an effective psychopath? Convincing you they were normal enough to get into the car with? To go home with?

To go to bed with.

A shudder of horror racked her body at the thought, incongruent with the shudders she had felt the night before. Her mind played tricks on her, imagining alternative scenarios of a morning that might have been. Would she would have shown her true colours? A darker side of herself? Might she have done something in the comfort of her own apartment that would have given the game away?

Or would she have woken up, made them both breakfast and continued with the elaborate lie until she was able to draw Kate in even closer?

So many questions and there were no answers. That was the hardest part of this whole mess, Kate knew. There couldn't be any answers without asking Hayley outright. After everything she had read, she wasn't sure she would be able to believe her words regardless. The plans and dreams she had enjoyed yesterday of their relationship developing, growing into something unique and special, lay shattered all around her.

The memory of her kisses felt like a betrayal, bringing back those words with them. I love you.

Kate had fallen in love with a ghost. A spectre. As real as if she had brought the perfect woman to life with nothing more than the power of her imagination.

The last information about Rachael Taylor Chapman's whereabouts was from an article years ago. Even then, it had been purely speculation, naming somewhere in Southern Francee. She had disappeared once her most recent court action had been completed and the libel award had been made. Fallen off the face of the planet and landed back as someone else, behind a bar in a sleepy little foreign town.

The face in the pictures from back then was haunted. Haunted and hunted. Of that, Kate was sure. But was she haunted by her own guilt, or haunted by her own foolishness for believing in her father? That was the real question. That and the question of what Kate was going to do next.

Hayley's fake life had been convincing. There was every chance Kate was the only person who knew the answer to where Rachael Taylor Chapman was. If she wasn't really innocent, as so many of the tabloids had indicated, then it would almost be a public service to let people know where she was. After all, Kate had no way of knowing if she was really the first person Hayley had allowed herself to be with, or if she was the last in a long line of girls who came through the town and disappeared, presumed moved on to other things.

Perhaps Pablo really did know the truth and the backpacker's hostel was an elaborate facade to lure more young women in? Didn't serial killers sometimes band together? She'd watched a documentary on it when she was at university, late at night when there was nothing else on TV, eating a bowl of microwave ramen noodles and thinking how stupid people were to allow themselves to get into that kind of situation in the first place.

She shook the thought from her head. That was insane. She was letting the midday heat and her imagination get the better of her, that was all. Pablo wouldn't hurt a fly.

Strange she could make that assumption of him, but the doubts about Hayley would not leave her. But Pablo hadn't been in her bed - twice - and certainly hadn't wormed his way into a space inside her heart.

As she reached the spot where the two of them had shared such an amazing time only a week or so before, Kate knew she had to make a decision. Did she give Hayley a chance to explain herself or did she walk away now and leave the whole thing behind?

Even if she could bring herself to believe that Hayley was telling the truth, could she ever get over such a cruel and brutal betrayal?

CHAPTER NINETEEN

As the sun gave way from noon to late afternoon, Hayley became increasingly frantic. She had spent every moment of the day looking for Kate. She hadn't eaten or even taken a drink of water and she'd rendered herself virtually delirious in the heat.

Her first port of call had been obvious. She had raced up the hill to Pablo's, pushing her old car harder than it had ever been driven before. It had screamed as she took the hill too fast, threatening to slide on the gravel when she had hit the turn at the top. Fear and determination had kept her on the road and she had pulled onto the makeshift car park next to Pablo's hostel with a grind of brakes and gears.

He had rushed out to see who was driving like a fool on his property and had been clearly surprised to see it was Hayley. He had asked her what was wrong, but when the words came out of her mouth, she was talking with speed and panic. He had shook his head and she had pushed past him instead of trying to explain herself. She had run down the hallway to Kate's room and banged on the door, not caring who she woke up in the process.

The door hadn't opened straight away. She hadn't expected it to. It didn't matter. She was prepared to keep banging on it until Kate came out and faced her. She beat her fist against the wood again, ignoring Pablo's protestations.

'She's not in.' A voice behind her had stilled her fist. She'd turned around to see Chad there, standing in his shorts and giving her a hard look. 'What did you do?' His Californian accent wasn't soft as she expected. It had a thread of steel cut through it and she knew he'd seen Kate that morning.

Asking her what she had done gave her the glimmer of hope that at least he didn't know the truth. If nothing else, Kate hadn't betrayed her to him. 'Where is she?'

'I don't know. And even if I did, then why would I tell you?'

'Please, if you do know then tell me.'

'Why did she come back crying this morning?'

'I can't tell you. I'm sorry. I just need to know that she's okay.'

'I can't tell you that. When I saw her, she sure as hell didn't look it.'

'I have to talk to her. Please, just tell me where she is.'

'And I've told you, I don't know. She took my scooter and went for a ride. That was about an hour ago. She hasn't come back yet.' He folded his arms across his bare chest and stared her down. Men like him hadn't intimidated her for a long time but she didn't care about putting him in his place. He'd told her everything he knew.

Hayley had pushed past Pablo and walked down the coolness of the hall back into the bright daylight. From her position on the hill, she looked around, but she knew it was futile. Unless Kate was on her way back, then she would have no way of spotting her in the distant traffic moving through town. Instead, she would have to drive around and hope to find her. Serendipity wasn't much of a plan, but it was all she had.

She ignored Pablo's pleas for an explanation and then his furious curses as she got in the car and turned the key in the ignition. She'd pulled away with another squeal, driving with one eye on the road and one eye out for any bike that might be Kate. She'd driven back to the bar in the hope that Kate had decided to return to her. She must have questions, Hayley reasoned. It would make sense for her to come back, even if it was just to yell at her for all the lies that had tumbled so easily from her lips.

Hi, I'm Kate.

Hi. Hayley. Hayley Jones.

From the very first, it had been an untruth. One that she was so used to telling that it had never even crossed her mind at that moment it was a lie.

There hadn't been any sign of the scooter or of Kate. She'd driven around town in an endless loop. Starting with cafes and bars, she had cruised the streets looking at the parking spots for anything that could indicate Kate was there.

Nothing.

She'd given up and gone to the beach. There were tourists lining it up and down, baking themselves various shades of red and brown in the sun, but no one that made her heart jump with the hope it could be Kate.

It had been nearly 2pm when the realisation had hit her that Kate might have made her way to the park. It was the perfect place to escape from the world. The first place they had gone together alone after that ill-fated night of passion.

It was a risk. The park was a long drive in the wrong direction if she was wrong. Her gut told her that it would be where she would find Kate. She would take the chance.

Now, silhouetted against the horizon, she could see Kate sitting on the rocky outcrop and was glad she'd followed the courage of her convictions. Her shorts had ripped on the fence as she'd climbed it. She'd cursed out loud but no one had been around to hear her.

They were alone.

If Kate wanted to shout and scream then she could. Hayley didn't have to fear the words reaching the ears of others.

The sound of her feet scuffing on the dirt track caught Kate's ears and she turned around. Her eyes were hidden behind sunglasses, but trails through the dust on her cheeks told Hayley she'd been crying. Fear made her pause in her steps.

Kate didn't run. Kate didn't even stand. She just turned away.

Somehow, that felt worse.

'Can I sit with you?' the words caught in Hayley's throat. For a long minute, there was no response. Then, the slightest nod.

Hayley took a deep breath and walked the rest of the

way, closing the distance between them. She sat down next to Kate - not too close - and stared off into the horizon with her.

The day had been spent running towards this moment. Now it was here and she didn't even know how to begin. In all her nightmares when this happened, she never hung around. She never explained. She ran.

In her nightmares, she woke with her legs kicking the sheets and her heart pounding as she made her escape from those who could hurt her.

In reality, she'd started running, but not away. She'd run to Kate and despite everything else, it had felt like the right thing to do.

'I know you know.' It was a pointless way to start, but it was the only thing she could come up with.

'I know.' It was a pointless confirmation too. They were at this point and they both knew what had led them here. But what else could she say? She couldn't make it go away. She couldn't undo the events of the midnight hours and everything that followed.

'I'm sorry.' It meant little, but she had to say it.

'Why did you do it?'

'You're going to have to be more specific than that.' Hayley shrugged. There were so many things she could have done differently in hindsight. Not that she would necessarily change things if she could turn the clock back. To do so would mean never knowing Kate's touch and despite everything else, that seemed too high a price to pay.

'Why did you let me fall in love with you?' It was a choking, angry accusation and the one thing she could not defend herself against. She had tried to warn Kate from the beginning that falling in love with her was the one thing she shouldn't do. There were many other things to apologise for. To explain. But Kate's first angry accusation was actually aimed towards herself.

'I didn't want you to fall in love with me. Just like I didn't want to fall in love with you. That was why I left you on that first morning.'

'Then why didn't you make me stay away?'

'Unless I'm mistaken, you wouldn't listen to me when I told you that was exactly what you should do. I tried to stop you from pushing. I couldn't stop you. You insisted on making me fall in love with you too. Bringing me to places like this. Taking me to the most amazing dinner last night. I told you over and over that I couldn't be in a relationship with you. But you kept coming to me and the more I got to know you, the harder it was to stop the way I felt. I desperately wanted to feel nothing for you. And it hurts me to say that as much as it hurts you,' she added at Kate's renewed sobs.

'Why didn't you say no?'

'I should have been more forceful. I get that. But I didn't want you to hate me either. I didn't want you to think I was nothing but a cold-hearted, mean-spirited bitch who had used you for sex one night. Because that wasn't what it was. That isn't who I am either. I wanted you to see the real me, even though I knew it was dangerous.'

'You were lying to me the whole time.'

'Was I? Really? Nothing I *did* was a lie. My name, my past? Those things are set in stone and I can't change them. I didn't tell you the truth about either of them, but can you blame me for that? They're not who I am any more. The person you saw, the person you spent the night with last night, that was the real me. The things we did together were with the real me. Not anything you've found out about me since.'

'That's easy for you to say.'

'Believe it or not, it's really not easy at all. I haven't spoken to anyone other than my lawyer about this for nearly a decade.'

'Pablo doesn't know?'

'No. What could I gain from telling him? Every additional person who knows is someone who could let the secret out. I've fought so hard to become Hayley Jones. I can't take the risk.'

'Would you ever have told me?'

'I don't know,' Hayley shrugged. She didn't. The future was something she tried not to think about. It was easier to get through each day when you didn't have hopes and dreams of things that might never happen. 'I could lie to you and say that of course I would, but I don't know. I would have probably spent each day putting it off and telling myself that I would tell you tomorrow.'

'Then I suppose I should be glad that I've found out now.' There was bitterness in Kate's voice and although it hurt, Hayley couldn't blame her.

'I can't take back the things I didn't tell you, but I can be honest with you now.' She spread out her palms in apology. 'That's the best I can do. You can ask me anything. I won't lie to you anymore.'

'How am I supposed to believe you?' It wasn't a question Hayley was sure she would ever have the answer to.

'I don't know. I can't make that decision for you. If you choose not to then I'll let you just walk out of my life. I guess you're going to do that anyway.'

'If you think I'm going to walk away, then why are you here?'

'To try and explain, I guess. To beg you not to tell anyone. There's not much I can do to stop you. But if I have a chance to explain, then perhaps you won't let anyone know. You'll keep my secret.'

'Why should I?'

'Because I'm not sure I can go through it all again.' She'd promised Kate honesty and that was it. 'I'm not trying to guilt trip you into silence. How much did you read? I'm assuming that's what you did. I know there's a lot of stuff about me out there.'

'A lot,' Kate admitted. 'More than I should have.'

'Then you'll know that there are plenty of journalists out there who thought I was guilty too. It didn't matter that I was fifteen when I found out like everyone else. That I'd been a kid when he - my father - was doing all those things. I'd spent enough time with him to know better, that was what they thought.'

'Did your mother know?'

'She always said she didn't. I want to believe her. I really do. But killing herself when she did, how can I really be sure? She might have done it because she couldn't bear that she had loved a man who was a monster. Or she could have known and once the guilt came out she couldn't live with herself anymore. I was too young to ask proper questions then. I was in shock.'

As she bared her soul for the first time since her therapist had sat her down on a couch and helped her turn her life around, she realised it was true. If she'd been the age she was now when she found out, then the shock would have stopped her from thinking straight anyway. There would have been louder recriminations as an adult, more accusations, she was sure of that. But questions that got to the heart of the truth? Probably not.

'So you don't know then.' Kate was turning the question and its implications over in her brain, Hayley could tell.

'No. I never did and I never will. If I had to guess, I would say she had suspicions that he was sleeping around while he was on those long road trips. With adult eyes, I know what people get up to when they're away from home. I see it in the bar all the time. Perhaps he had a temper with her that I never saw. But I have to believe that she didn't know until we all did. If I don't, well,' Hayley paused, her fists clenching back and forth, 'then I have to live with the fact that not only did she abandon me to a shitty life to deal with on my own, but that she was partly responsible too.'

'But didn't you get help?'

'That's what people think, don't they? That people just have to ask for help. That it's out there if you need it. Let me tell you, no one cares about the kid of a killer. Not even the authorities. People care less when they suspect you might have got away with it too. People said it to my face. Called me a murderer in the streets. I was fifteen. They were grown men. So no, Kate, there was no help.'

'I'm sorry.' Despite the tears, despite the circumstances

that had led them to this moment, Kate sounded genuine.

'So am I. I tried, really hard, to turn my life around. Just to survive. I told myself that my mother would be his last victim, not me. I wouldn't do what she did. I wouldn't give him the satisfaction of having another life on his hands. But it was so, so hard.

Every day, it was all about survival. Not about being happy. Not about going out with friends. Not about getting a girlfriend. The thought of that terrified me. I worried that only a crazy girl would want to go out with me. One I couldn't trust. I didn't want an unhappy relationship and that seemed the only one open to me. So instead, I focused on getting through it and resigned myself to a life alone.'

'So no one night stands? That part was true?'

'It was true. Even out here, once I was certain that everyone believed I was Hayley Jones, I never took the chance. I didn't want even want anyone. It was more important to finally feel safe, even if that meant being alone forever.'

'Then I came along.'

'Then you came along,' Hayley agreed, 'and changed everything. After years of telling myself that I was never going to get love, never find it, I think I have. Turns out,' she barked out a bitter laugh,' I was right all along. I might have found it, but now I'm not going to keep it after all. I still don't get to be happy. I'm not blaming you for that,' she added quickly, in case Kate thought she was trying to apply the guilt again. 'I'm really not. But now you know what it was like for me, all I can do is beg you not to tell anyone else. Let me live out my days here.'

'You don't have to beg,' Kate said. She didn't move closer. The tears had dried, but she was still looking out over the horizon rather than back at her. 'I just don't know what to do.'

'Neither do I. But you saw what they were like back then. Can you imagine what it will be like for me if they find me again. It's been twenty years since the trial. That's how long I've been running from this. Twenty years.'

'I was four.' It was a statement of fact, but a sharp reminder of the differences between them.

'I know. Too young to even know what twenty years feels like. This is bad enough, I don't need you to remind me of that.'

'I didn't mean it like that,' sighed Kate. 'I just meant that twenty years for me is a lifetime. How have you managed to never tell anyone?'

'It was hard. But I knew what the alternative was. Every time I wanted to let someone know, every time I just wanted to stop lying, I knew that if I did, Hayley Jones would be gone. The bar would be gone. I wouldn't have any friends again. I took the money from the libel case and I saw my chance to escape. I took it. Every day, I look back, waiting for the past to catch up with me. This morning, I guess it did.'

'So why did you invite me back last night?'

'Because since I met you, things have stopped making sense. I know what I should do and I know what I want to do. You had a way of making me forget that this might happen. Last night, all I knew was that I wanted to stop fighting the feelings I have for you. I wanted to let you in. So I did. As we walked up the stairs I thought about changing my mind. About sending you away, for both of our sakes. But then you were behind me and I was too weak. I needed you so much that my brain stopped working.'

'I don't know what I can do to change this.' Kate looked helpless again and it broke Hayley's heart when another tear rolled down her face.

'You can't change it. It is what it is. If things could be changed, then I would have changed them long ago. So all I can do is plead with you to give me a chance to carry on here. You were going to leave anyway. Go off on your adventures. I was always going to stay. So perhaps our hearts have just broken sooner, but they were going to anyway, right?'

As she said the words, she knew they were the truth.

But unlike the lies scattered through her life, the truth didn't make the pain easier to bear.

CHAPTER TWENTY

Kate had listened to Hayley's confession and her heart reached out to her. She'd come here to be alone, but when Hayley had arrived, it had taken away the decision about whether or not to hear her out. It had forced her to listen. When she'd heard her approach, she'd been too tired to walk away.

Tired was the word. Even in the heat of the summer tropics, she didn't think she'd ever felt this drained. Now, with the full story running around her head, she only felt more exhausted. Hayley had promised to be honest with her at last. She'd given her the chance to ask questions.

But did she believe the answers?

'Why did you choose here?' she said, looking out at the mountain ridge in the distance.

'What?'

'Out of all the places in the world, why here? I'm just wondering.'

'Oh,' Hayley paused and, after a few moments,

shrugged. 'Would you believe me if I said it was the first place I got to where I felt like I could stop running? It really was as simple as that. It felt like the place I should be. I knew that if I wanted to start a life somewhere as someone else, then I needed to do something. The bar was for sale. It was cheap and I could afford it. Fate, I guess.'

'That was it?'

'Yes. I think so. It wasn't about being close to the ocean. Or being in a hot country, although after the miserable weather in England, it was a nice change. Even the winters here are great. But when it comes down to it, the bar is what I needed and what has kept me here ever since.'

'Were the news stories true? Did you really get that much from the settlement?'

'Yes. It sounds like a lot, but it's not enough to never work again. Not really. Besides, working behind a bar was the only thing I knew. The only person who ever took a chance on me was someone who owned a pub. I knew the ropes of customer service. The actual running of the business? Not so much. But it was more than I knew about anything else and the main point was to do something.' Hayley sounded as tired as she was. The truth, when spoken aloud, was more mundane that Kate's imagination had led her to believe.

'I think I would have wanted to relax for a while. Chill at the beach.' Kate realised she was putting herself in Hayley's shoes as a twenty-four year old. When she pushed the bitterness and betrayal aside and allowed empathy in, she could see how hard it must have been.

'Oh no. That was the last thing I wanted.'

'Really?' Kate was surprised. It had sounded so hard for Hayley up to that point. Surely a chance to stop would have been amazing.

'I didn't want to do anything that gave me time to think. I needed to keep my hands and my mind busy. Otherwise, I'd never really leave it behind. It would be the only thing I still had in my life. The bar caused me no end of stress in that first year, but it was the most liberating feeling. It was stress that I could do something about. Problems I could solve. That was when I understood that stress and fear were different things.'

'Has the fear gone now?'

'The fear never goes. Not fully. Certainly not today.'

'What if I decide to tell someone?' The words were out before Kate really had chance to make a conscious decision. She watched as Hayley ran her hands up and down her shorts, wiping the sweat away. Kate noticed that somehow they'd been ripped.

It was a foolish test. She didn't even know why she was doing it. If Hayley was anything like her father, then Kate herself was a prime victim. No one knew she was here. No one even knew about this place other than Hayley. Her article wasn't scheduled to post until next week, set up using Chad's technology so she didn't have to worry about it. So she could focus on the time she'd been planning to spend with Hayley instead.

No one would hear her scream or cry for help.

What the hell was she playing at, making threats and testing her? The silence grew and she frantically thought of a way to back out of the statement.

'Then I can't stop you,' Hayley finally said and Kate

saw a tear fall. Her back straightened. Some kind of resolve, a strength born of necessity took over. 'All I ask is that you give me a day or two to sort things out. The bar. Marco's family depend on his paycheck. Give me a chance to say goodbye to Pablo.'

'If I told someone, you wouldn't stay?'

'Of course not. This place has become my home. These people have become my friends. They don't need their lives upended by a media circus. It will be bad enough anyway, but at least if I'm not around then it will be over for them quicker.'

Kate wasn't sure she wanted to know what 'not around' meant. If it was somewhere else, a new location, or something more sinister. Hayley brushed the tears away and stood. 'I really am sorry for everything.'

'Sit down,' Kate reached up and took her hand, pulling her back to a seated position on the rough grass beside her. Closer this time. 'I'm not going to tell anyone.'

'You're not?'

'No. I guess,' Kate couldn't bring herself to admit she'd tested Hayley to see if she was a psychopath after all. 'I guess I just had to know what you would do if I did. I don't want to ruin your life.'

'Even if I've ruined yours?'

'It's not ruined. I'm confused as hell, but it's not ruined. I just wasn't ready for this, you know? I thought we would keep seeing each other and last night…last night was special. The first time we were together was amazing but last night felt like something more. Like it was the start of something that would last. Then I fell asleep feeling one thing and left this morning feeling something else entirely.

It's been a hell of a day.'

'I can't imagine how it feels.'

'I've been dealing with it for a day,' Kate shrugged. 'You've been living with it for two decades. I think you know how it feels.'

'But it should never have been yours to bear, not even for one day.'

'If everything you've told me is true, then it shouldn't have been yours either.' Kate had thought her parents had given her a hard time over her life choices, but it was nothing compared to this. To her surprise, it was Hayley's mother who angered her the most. Her father, after reading what he had done to those girls, scared and repulsed her. Sometimes, there was just evil in the world. That was what he was at his core. Hayley's mother had abandoned Hayley to fight for herself. To grow up and deal with the horror and torment alone. That, on some strange level, Kate found more unforgivable.

'Do you believe me?' it was almost inaudible and childlike in its hope. Kate looked at the woman next to her and finally understood the look that had sometimes crossed her face. The one that she'd struggled to define. She'd thought it was because she was being hard and distant. Now she saw it for the exact opposite: vulnerability.

The question lay there between them and Kate knew that to lie at this point would make her no better than Hayley. If they were to stand any kind of chance, then they both had to be completely honest with each other from this point forward.

'I'm not sure,' she confessed in the end. 'I want to

believe you. So much.'

'But?'

'It's a lot to take in. I guess I feel like I have to get to know you all over again.'

'I won't be any different. I've been the person I am now all along. I don't want to go back to being her. So if the person you've been spending time with isn't the person you want to be with, then don't expect it to change.'

'But she is the person I want to be with.' Kate swallowed. 'Did you mean it?'

'Which bit?'

'The bit before. When you said you loved me.'

'Oh, that.' Hayley fiddled awkwardly with a blade of grass in front of her. Kate could see a blush growing on her cheeks. After all the things she'd confessed, all the deepest darkest secrets, it appeared this was the hardest thing of all for her to talk about.

'Yes, that.' Kate smiled. It felt nice to have an alternative to the tears and the sadness that had gripped her all day.

'Yes, I meant it. I don't expect you to feel the same way, obviously. With everything else that's happened today, you probably didn't need to hear that too.'

'I want to know the truth, remember. If that's how you feel then I know that last night wasn't just sex for you either.'

'It really wasn't.'

'I'm glad.' Kate knew she should say something about her feelings in reciprocation. But right now, the words weren't there. She'd spent weeks falling in love with Hayley. She'd been there for awhile. After that first night, she'd known on some level that Hayley was the one for her. Part of her held back now. If she told her today, with everything else that was happening, it would get lost amongst the other emotions.

Besides, if Kate couldn't bring herself to make it work once they left the isolation of the park, then Hayley would know she'd lost another person who'd loved her too.

'So what now?' as if sensing her thoughts, Hayley looked backwards towards the entrance. Her shoulders were still rounded in defeat. Both of them were so very tired.

Kate had left home to travel because her life had been at a crossroads. For the first time since she stepped onto the plane, she was at another. Right from the start, she had known that a relationship with Hayley wouldn't be easy. They lived such different lives. But she had never expected it to be this hard either. The Kate of yesterday felt young and idyllic. A dreamer. The Kate of today had become a different person. More realistic. More aware.

'Now, we go home,' Kate stood and pulled Hayley up with her. The two of them were close. Kate didn't let go of her hand. 'I need to return Chad's bike. I *really* need to have a shower. Then, perhaps, I could come over tonight?'

'You want to?' Hayley smiled at her and Kate felt her heart contract. Here, away from everything, she could pretend for a few moments that they would deal with everything else tomorrow.

'If you'll have me.'

'Always.'

Kate felt a familiar flutter in her stomach at that smile. She had no idea what she was going to do tomorrow, but as she closed the distance between them, all she cared about was the moment. She felt Hayley's lips against her own, tentative at first. The kiss was soft, not imbued with the passion that had marked their previous times together. As Hayley reached up and stroked her face, this kiss felt more like a promise.

CHAPTER TWENTY-ONE

Four months later...

'I have no idea how I'm meant to get the rest of my stuff in there.' Hayley looked at the backpack in the middle of the bed. Kate had assured her it was big enough, but it was already two thirds full. She'd always considered herself a person of few possessions. Always ready to run. Now, faced with over a decade of accumulated bits and pieces, she was starting to see she was wrong.

'Just take what you need,' Kate lay on the bed next to the bag, typing on her laptop. 'At least you don't have all this stuff to fit in your carry on as well.' She gestured to the laptop and camera at her side. Over the past few months, Hayley had finally begun to understand what it all meant as Kate patiently showed her how she built her career online.

The implicit understanding that they had come to, of course, was that in order for Kate to continue to do so, then she needed to get back out into the world and visit more places. Her list of admin tasks had dwindled to nothing as she had worked through them at the table in Hayley's apartment.

With each new piece of information Hayley had learned, the fear of Kate leaving had grown stronger.

The previous few months had been far from easy. The two of them had tiptoed around each other in the beginning. The night after telling Kate everything, the two of them had lain in her bed, close but barely touching. It had been tense and strange, until a week later when they had an explosive fight over something so insignificant neither of them could remember what it was now. It was the first time Hayley had yelled in years. It shocked and terrified her.

But it had also cleared the air. Kate had walked out. She'd returned a few hours later.

That night, they had made love again for the first time since Kate had found out who she really was.

The following day, she'd moved down from Pablo's with all her bags. Hayley had seen her in the doorway and knew that Kate had finally made the decision to try to make it work.

For the first time in twenty years, Hayley had weathered the media storm of that anniversary with someone by her side. They hadn't talked much during those days. Hayley's nightmares returned and she woke to find Kate's arms around her, holding her close and whispering that everything would be okay.

Place by place, Kate reintroduced her to the world via a thirteen inch laptop screen. Places Hayley never even knew existed. Places that excited Kate in a way that this sleepy little town never could.

Each day had felt like it was inching closer to the day when Kate would leave. But, in the way that Hayley had come to recognise as her modus operandi, she had sown the seeds to convince Hayley that, just maybe, when Kate left, she didn't need to be left behind.

Now there was a backpack on the bed in front of her and she felt the strangest combination of elation and terror she had ever experienced in her life.

Between them, they had weighed up the risks. It wasn't as if Hayley had an actual criminal record she needed to declare, but that didn't mean they would take any unnecessary risks. Kate had been planning to go back to London, but Hayley vetoed that without discussion. Kate could go alone if she wanted and then come back for her, but she wouldn't be going anywhere near England. The further away from where she grew up, the better.

That was when Kate had suggested heading back to south East Asia. She still needed to check out the rest of Cambodia. Why not?

That was the question really. Why not?

When Hayley realised she didn't have a good answer for that any more, she had agreed to go. Despite arguing she was far too old to become a backpacker, she had nevertheless allowed Kate to spin her web of adventure until she was caught like a fly with no chance of escape. A whispered midnight conversation had opened her heart to the possibility that the rest of her life could really be spent with the woman she had loved like a dream from the start.

She stared out the window. An adventure was about to

begin, but she would miss this town. The bar. The first place she had felt happy since childhood.

'Any regrets?' Kate's arms slipped around her waist. Hayley hadn't heard her get up from the bed.

'No. No regrets. Not yet.'

'I don't want you to have any ever. Remember, no matter what happens, you'll always have this place to come back to. Pablo will take good care of it.'

'I know.' Kate was right. Pablo was a safe pair of hands to leave her livelihood in. With the hostel up and running, a new manager in place, Pablo was looking for another challenge. The bar was the perfect opportunity for him to turn his hand to running a new business whilst still spending time in one of his favourite places. Besides, Marco would really be doing the important tasks, but Pablo didn't need to know that.

Hayley had promised she would come back when they'd talked about it and he'd agreed to take it on. Now, with everything about to change, she wasn't sure if she ever would. It was a new thing for her, thinking about the future. It didn't come naturally and often her mind attempted to shut down the thoughts when she had them. Every day she spent with Kate, the desire to do more than simply make it through the day safely grew.

There had even been talk of heading back over to Australia next year so Kate could see her family. The meaning was clear. The two of them would go and Hayley would be introduced to her parents at last.

For all her difficulties thinking long term, Kate appeared to have no such qualms.

#

The sun had begun to set when they stood at the front of the bar one final time. Hayley had made Pablo promise there would be no elaborate farewell. She wanted to sneak off into the night, very much in the same way as she had snuck into the town all those years ago.

Two backpacks, full to bursting, stood next to them as Kate took Hayley's hand in hers. There was no need for words. Hayley took a few minutes to memorise this view. In all the years she had been here, she had never seen things so clearly. The calm of the ocean. The dry heat at the end of the day. The sound of laughter and enthusiastic Spanish chatter filtering out from the bar behind her. It had surrounded her every single day of this life and had become part of who she was.

The last flight of the day would be the first flight of their new lives together. The next sunset she watched would be halfway around the world and a whole other life away from the one she had stumbled upon all those years ago. Kate had assured her it would be different, but just as beautiful.

The sound of a car pulling up drew her from her thoughts. The taxi had arrived for them. She felt the weight of Pablo's hand on her shoulder. She turned and, for the first time in their friendship, fully embraced him. She thought she saw a tear in his eye, but he wiped it away before she could comment. Instead, he pulled from her grip and picked up their bags to load into the car.

For a moment, she knew she could change her mind. She felt the fear and enormity of what lay ahead grip her heart and squeeze.

'Ready?' asked Kate. There was so much hope and joy in her eyes that Hayley knew she would never be able to deny her anything. At her touch, the pain in her heart grew a little less.

'Ready,' she nodded, taking a deep breath.

She knew it was the truth. From the moment Kate had walked into her life, she'd been brought back to life. With each kiss they had shared, she finally understood what living meant. It was time to stop being afraid of the world.

It was time to live in it again.

ABOUT THE AUTHOR

C.K. Martin is a British writer of mostly - but not exclusively - lesbian fiction. She loves writing character-driven stories, so you'll find her books in the romance, crime, thriller and fantasy genres. She believes that realistic, diverse and engaging characters shouldn't come at the expense of great plots - readers deserve to have both. If you enjoy her characters in one genre, then you'll find similar heroines in the others if you feel like branching out. Discover detectives, vampires, gangsters and runaways, all looking for their happy ending.

When she's not writing, she can usually be found with her nose in a book (or pressed against the Kindle screen). Her third biggest passion in life is travel, so although she's based in England, for much of the year you won't find her there. Instead she'll be hanging out with her wife in some amazing city or, more likely, at the beach.

You can get in touch with the author by email ckmartin.author@gmail.com, or follow on twitter @CKMauthor. For more frequent updates, visit http://www.ckmartin.com/

Printed in Great Britain
by Amazon